BILLIONAIRE BAD BOY

A BEDDING THE BILLIONAIRE NOVELLA

LAURA LEE

This book is dedicated to any women who has been a victim of rumors or slut shaming. You're strong, you're smart, and you're beautiful—inside and out.

Anyone who thinks otherwise, can suck it.

NOW

GABBIE

"Oh, Gabs, I just heard the news. I'm so sorry."

I look up as Lila, my best friend since high school, walks through the door of my bakery, Sweet Temptations.

"Um...what news? And why are you here so early?"

Lila's eyes widen. "You haven't heard?"

I place one last cupcake in the display case. "I hear lots of things but I have a feeling you have something specific in mind. Hey, flip the open sign for me, will you?"

"Shit," she mutters as she does what I've asked.

"Spit it out, lady," I say. "I have to bring out the tarts before the rush begins."

She sighs. "Someone bought the space next door. My office brokered the deal and the client signed on the dotted line yesterday. I just heard this morning when I dropped by to pick up some fliers and I drove straight here."

Lila is a realtor in one of Santa Monica's biggest firms. At only thirty years old, she's done pretty well for herself. Let's face it; real estate in California isn't cheap wherever you go, but especially not anywhere near the ocean. Higher sales prices mean higher commissions. The only reason I managed to afford my place was because I spent a couple years hosting shows on the Cooking Network which led to some endorsement deals.

Two years ago, I became painfully aware of how fast Hollywood can turn on you and just wanted to get back to doing what I love: crafting baked goods. So, here I am, running a shop in Santa Monica, only a few minutes' walk from the pier. Like clockwork, tourists and locals begin lining up around 8:00 in the morning and don't stop until I've run out of inventory for the day.

"Do you know what it's going to be? Please don't tell me it's another bike rental shop. Lord knows we have enough of those."

Lila shakes her head slowly. "Nope. Definitely no bikes involved."

I frown. "Why are you being so damn cryptic? Just tell me what you know, Lila."

She opens her mouth to reply but the bell dings as my first customer of the day walks in. Lila's eyes widen when she sees the man strutting through the door while my eyes narrow into slits. What in the hell is *he* doing here?

None other than Ethan Baldwin, celebrity chef extraordinaire, also the biggest asshole I've ever met, walks up to the counter.

Ethan gives me a salacious grin. "Gabriela, nice to see you again."

"I wish I could say the same. What are you doing here?"

He ignores my question and looks around the small space. I take advantage of his inattention and look at *him*. Damn, it would be nice if he wasn't so good looking. With his dark, artfully tossed hair, tanned skin, and muscles for days, he's easily the most attractive man I've met in person. Seriously. I can't find a single physical imperfection, and believe me, we've spent enough time together for me to notice any. He's tall, too which doesn't seem fair in my opinion. This guy won the genetic lottery big time. Too bad he has to open his mouth and ruin it.

"This will do just fine," he muses.

What the hell is he talking about?

I grip the edge of the counter, holding back my rage. "What do you want, Ethan?" My tone is harsh and I'm not even sorry. After what this dickhead did to me, he's lucky I haven't smacked him yet.

His lips turn up at the corners. I refuse to acknowledge how full and kissable they are. "Now,

Gabbie, is that how you treat all of your customers? I can't imagine it's good for business."

I glare. "My business does just fine, not that it's any of your concern."

Lila is watching our exchange with avid interest. Honestly, I can't blame her. She knows my less than pleasant history with this man—hell, half the world probably does. If our roles were reversed, I would be fascinated, too.

Ethan rubs his stupidly square jaw, the light stubble making a scratching sound. "Now, that's where you're wrong, Gabs. Your business *is* my concern."

How dare he use my nickname? That's reserved solely for people I like. "How do you figure?"

His light blue eyes twinkle with mischief as a smile stretches across his face. "Because, *neighbor*, you're my number one competitor."

CHAPTER TWO

THEN

ETHAN

"Ethan, I'd like you to meet your fellow judge, Gabriela Martinez." .

I extend my hand. "Gabriela, it's a pleasure. I've seen your show...it's really great."

She shakes my hand with a smile. "Thank you. I'm a fan of your shows, too. And please, call me Gabbie."

Damn, this woman is even more stunning in person. Her pouty red lips would look perfect wrapped around my cock. And those curves...Jesus. She's definitely fit, as evidenced by her toned arms and sexy-as-fuck legs, but deliciously round in all the right places. This is a woman who takes care of herself but she's not afraid to eat. I've always appreciated having something to hold on to. Someone I'm not afraid I'd break during sex. In Hollywood, women are practically walking skeletons more often than not.

With her bronzed skin, truffle-colored eyes, and thick black hair, Gabbie Martinez could easily pass for Sofia Vergara's much younger sister. Fuck, it's going to take some serious effort keeping things professional when all I want to do is pull her into a room and fuck her senseless. And with the way she's looking at me right now, I'd say she wouldn't mind that one bit.

"So..." Eric, our producer, claps his hands together. "Now that introductions are out of the way, let's tour the set of *Baking Masters*, shall we?"

"Sure," Gabbie and I reply in unison.

I'd like to say I'm a gentleman, but sadly, I cannot. The entire time we walk around, I intentionally stay behind just enough to watch those curves in motion. My hands are itching to grab her ass like you wouldn't believe. Fuck, I can only imagine how those heart-shaped cheeks would feel in my palms as I took her from behind. At one point, Gabbie looks back and catches me red-handed. When she winks, then turns around and continues walking with a little extra sway in her hips, my dick jumps for joy. Then I remember the no fraternization clause in our contract and want to weep.

After several scandals involving hookups and harassment charges with judges or contestants, the network put a clause into all new contracts that prohibits amorous relationships of any kind. While a full season only takes about a month to film, there are auditions and promo work which can be time consuming. Both Gabbie and I are locked in for three seasons, twelve episodes each, so all things considered, we're talking at least nine months before I could ever act on this attraction to her.

I'm not sure if I'll make it nine hours.

CHAPTER THREE

THEN

GABBIE

"This is taking too damn long." I suppress a shiver as Ethan whispers in my ear."

I look at the digital timer on the wall. "They only have fifteen minutes left."

"Thank fuck," he says, a little too loudly. "I could really use a drink."

"Shh!" I whisper harshly.

"Why? Our mics are off." He chuckles and gestures to the three contenders currently baking their asses off. "Besides, they're too busy panicking to listen."

Each episode of *Baking Masters* has two rounds and the tasks become significantly more difficult in the second half. It's how we separate the amateurs from the real talent. Today, we challenged our remaining contestants to make gluten-free cupcakes, and they're required to incorporate beets into their recipe. By the panicked look on their faces, I'm guessing two of them have never worked with wheat flour alternatives, so this should be interesting. Unfortunately for them, the gluten-free fad doesn't seem to be going anywhere, especially not in L.A. Hell, you could probably rob a bank with a damn bagel in this town.

I nod toward the woman who seems to be struggling the most. "I'm sort of afraid to taste hers."

Ethan barks out a laugh. "I'm fucking terrified. But that's why they pay us the big bucks, right?"

"Right." I smirk. "I'll probably be ready for a drink afterwards, too. Maybe if I consume enough, my brain will purge the awful taste from my memory."

He bumps his shoulder into mine. "It's settled, then. We're getting shitfaced as soon as we get out of here."

I smile. "Deal."

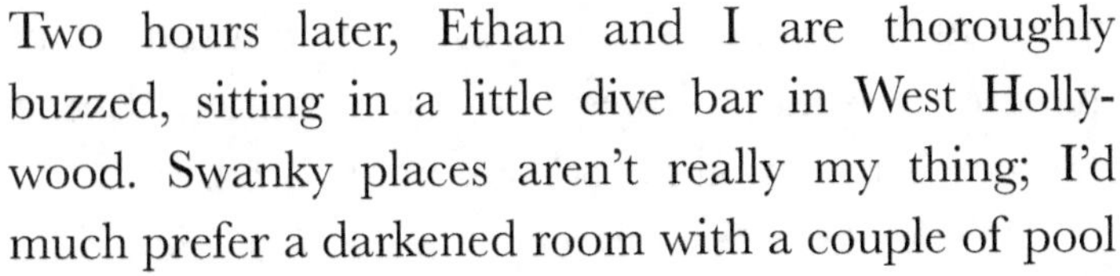

Two hours later, Ethan and I are thoroughly buzzed, sitting in a little dive bar in West Hollywood. Swanky places aren't really my thing; I'd much prefer a darkened room with a couple of pool tables. When I mentioned this to Ethan, he said he knew just the place. I've gotta give it to him—the man certainly delivered. The California sun is shining brightly outside, but the lighting in here is so dim, you can barely make out people's faces.

"So...you come here often?" I ask.

"Isn't that my line?" he laughs.

"Wiseass." I roll my eyes.

He takes a lengthy sip of whiskey. "I meet some buddies here a few times per month. It's a good place to go when I want to avoid recognition."

"Ah, the life of a superstar," I tease.

Ethan chuckles. "I'm not that big of a star."

I scoff. "Please. *I'm* not that big of a star. You? Not so much."

Sure, I'm occasionally recognized by a fan of my show, but my celebrity status is nowhere near Ethan's. The man looks like a freaking model so he's bound to draw attention regardless, but his face is definitely recognizable.

At only thirty-three, he's hosted four insanely popular shows, has published several bestselling cookbooks, opened bakeries on the Las Vegas Strip and in Times Square, and has made countless appearances on talk shows. Not to mention the fact that he's usually linked to some starlet. Ethan Baldwin is undoubtedly a household name.

He winks. "You'll get there, Gabbie. The camera fucking loves you and your ratings are always through the roof. It's only a matter of time before the rest follows."

My eyebrows pinch together. "I'm not sure if I'd want that."

Ethan tilts his head to the side. "What do you mean?"

I gesture to him. "The fame. Being a paparazzi magnet holds no appeal for me. If I want to go to the grocery store wearing sweats and without makeup, I can. When I date someone, I don't have to worry about trolls and their opinion on my relationship. I like my job, and the paychecks are certainly nice, but it's not my endgame, you know?"

He leans forward. "What *is* your endgame?"

I shrug. "Eventually, I'd love to open a place by the beach. Get up early, make pastries, or cupcakes, or whatever I'm in the mood to bake that day. Then close up shop when all the food's gone, go home, enjoy a nice glass of wine. If I'm lucky, I'll have someone waiting for me to get home so we can snuggle."

"Someone to snuggle with, huh?" Ethan lifts an eyebrow which is oddly sexy. "Anyone filling that role now?"

I smile. "Are you asking if I'm single, Mr. Baldwin?"

He flashes a blinding smile. "Why, yes, I think I am."

"And why are you so interested?"

Ethan hooks his foot around my ankle and his gaze becomes heated. "Because, Miss Martinez, I'm quite interested in *you*."

CHAPTER FOUR

THEN

GABBIE

"I've been dying to get my hands on you." Ethan grabs my ass with both hands to demonstrate.

I lift my shirt over my head and throw it on the floor. "Less talking, more kissing."

He offers me a cocky grin as he takes in my black lace bra. "It'd be my pleasure." Ethan moves the cups down and takes my right nipple into his mouth. I suppose I didn't specify *where* I wanted to be kissed.

I arch my back as he lavishes attention on the other breast. We barely made it through the door to my apartment before we started mauling each other. As pathetic as it sounds, this is already the best sexual experience of my life. I've only known this man for a couple of months but I can say with absolute certainty, I've never wanted anyone more.

Maybe it's the alcohol talking, but I couldn't care less about the clause in our contracts right now. The whole thing is asinine, in my opinion. We're both consenting adults. We should be able to get involved with whomever we want. If we decide to explore anything beyond tonight, we'll just have to keep it quiet until we've finished filming.

I shout when Ethan bites down on my nipple and sucks.

He releases me with a pop. "So fucking sexy."

I pull on his thick hair, drawing his eyes to mine. "Fuck me, Ethan. Now."

He groans. "Hold on, baby." He loops his arms behind my thighs, encouraging me to jump up and wrap around him. "Where's your bedroom?"

I moan when he nips the sensitive skin right below my ear. "Down the hall on the left."

We're walking blindly, too busy kissing to worry about things like coordination. After what seems like forever, we make it to my bedroom. Ethan deposits me on the mattress and removes his white button-down shirt followed by the t-shirt underneath. The process is painstakingly slow; it's obvious he's teasing me, building the anticipation.

"*Dios mío*," I whisper as he finally reveals his ridiculously sculpted core, one rippled muscle at a time. How this man bakes for a living and winds up with those abs, is beyond me. I couldn't pull that off if I exercised twenty-four/seven.

Ethan flashes a cocky smile as he pushes his black slacks down just enough to stroke his impressive length. "You like what you see, Gabbie?"

I bite my lower lip. "That depends."

He raises an eyebrow. "On what?"

"Whether or not you know how to use that thing."

He releases a surprised laugh and steps out of his pants, removing a foil square from his wallet. Ethan joins me on the bed, deftly removes the rest of my clothing, and lines his body up flush with mine. I moan shamelessly when he slides his cock against my slick flesh before resting his weight on top of me.

"I can assure you, Gabs, I definitely know what to do with it."

"Prove it."

His eyes flicker with mirth. "Gladly, honey."

CHAPTER FIVE

NOW

ETHAN

Nobody can perfect a pastry like yours truly. Cakes, pies, tarts, cannoli…you name it—I'm the master. On my twenty-fifth birthday, I opened my first store smack dab in the middle of Times Square. Two years later, another one on the Las Vegas Strip.

Having two wildly successful bakeries under my belt, I was offered my first show with the Cooking Network. When its ratings went through the roof, they gave me three more, cementing my place within the industry and adding to my already impressive net worth.

With my rise in fame came an endless supply of women. I never had trouble getting laid but this was on a whole other level. I had to practically beat them off with a zester strip, for Christ's sake.

Overall, life was pretty fucking great.

Until Gabriela Martinez happened, that is. No matter how hard I try, I can't get that woman out of my brain, which brings me to my current dilemma.

I severely underestimated my willpower when I came up with this whole plan. Gabbie's even more beautiful than she was two years ago. The entire time she was glaring at me and throwing attitude my way, all I could think about was how badly I wanted to remind her of a time when we got along *very* well. I didn't realize it until this morning, but I fucking miss those times. The last month we were forced to work together was so volatile, it overshadowed any of the good we'd shared.

Fuck.

When I told my realtor I wanted to open my next retail store in the L.A. area, she found several suitable locations. I almost closed on one, but when I discovered that the space immediately adjacent to Sweet Temptations was available, I took it as a sign. Gabbie once tried to shit all over my career for her personal gain, so I plan to return the favor.

Despite the fact that she's the only pastry chef I

know with talent that could rival mine, she's no match for the popularity of my brand. The second I open for business, all of her customers will come through my door instead. And when I successfully drive her company into the ground, she'll have no choice but to sell her property, which I'll quickly snag to double my square footage.

Does that make me a dick? Maybe. But as the saying goes, all's fair in love and war. And she may not know it yet, but Gabbie and I are *definitely* at war.

CHAPTER SIX

GABBIE

"We shouldn't be doing this here," I pant.

Ethan's grip tightens on my hip as he lightly bites down on my shoulder. "I know. But you make me feel like a goddamn teenager who can't control his hormones."

My chuckle transforms into a gasp when he grinds his erection into my stomach. "I'm serious, Ethan. If we get caught, they could sue us for breach of contract."

He releases his hold on me and pulls back. He combs his fingers through his thick hair and heaves a sigh. "You're right; I'm sorry."

I step away from the wall he had me up against and straighten the collar on his button-down shirt. "Hey, you have nothing to apologize for. I was an active participant, too."

His full lips turn up in the corners. "Now that I think about it, you did pretty much tackle me."

I shove his chest playfully. "I did not!"

Ethan laughs as he looks in the mirror, smoothing down his hair. "It's okay, Gabs. I tend to have this effect on women. I'm used to it."

I roll my eyes. "Ass."

He tilts my chin up with his forefinger and presses a soft kiss against my lips. "I'll take that as a compliment, baby."

I shake my head and smile. "You would."

Someone knocks on my dressing room door. "Gabbie, have you seen Ethan anywhere? We roll in ten and I can't find him."

"Shit," I whisper, pushing Ethan into my small closet before cracking the door open to face our director's assistant. "Hey, Maria. He knocked on my door a few minutes ago to let me know he was heading to his car real quick. Apparently, he left his phone in there."

Her brown eyes narrow in suspicion but she nods anyway. "We need you on set."

"Sure...of course. Let me just use the restroom and I'll be right out."

I shut the door and turn the lock before she has the chance to respond. Taking a deep breath, I open the closet. "That was too close. We can't keep doing this, Ethan."

Ethan and I have been...dating, for lack of a

better word, for the last four months. Against my better judgement, I let my hormones lead the way because I'd never been so viscerally attracted to a man before. Call me crazy, but I felt compelled to explore that, despite the risks. The sex is amazing—best I've ever had—but the more I get to know him, the more his personality shines through. And that's the part that's pulling me in the most.

He's constantly making me laugh or smile. When we are intimate, he treats my body with nothing short of reverence, even when the sex is filthy. When we're baking together—which we like to do sometimes after filming is done for the day—he's always challenging me, but he's surprisingly humble enough to accept my suggested tweaks. I have a sneaking suspicion that I'm the only one who can get away with that though.

As if all those reasons weren't enough, he's insanely smart and driven, always extremely attractive traits in my book. And he's one of the few people I've met in this town that isn't blinded by all the glimmer and glitz of Hollywood.

I know we've only known each other a short time, but I can honestly see myself having a future with Ethan. We have such vastly different backgrounds though, I often wonder if that would pose a problem. Ethan was raised in Bel Air, a neighborhood known for its wealth and lack of diversity. While I was surviving the Inglewood public school system, he attended posh private schools. At fifteen, I was washing dishes part-time to help keep food on our table. His biggest worry was probably deciding which girl he was going to feel up over the weekend.

What would his family think of our relationship? As advanced as we've become as a society, racism and classism are still very much in full effect. Ours is a nation built by hard-working immigrants who came to this country with nothing more than the shirts on their backs. I think people forget that all too often. Maybe I'm worrying for nothing, but when you're subjected to the harsh reality of it during your formative years, I think my wariness is justified.

Ethan steps forward and wraps his big body around me, jolting me out of my reverie. "If you'd come home with me again, we wouldn't have to resort to sneaking around the studio."

I pull back and shake my head. "You know that wouldn't work. Not while all the photographers are so hot on your trail." He opens his mouth to say something but I hold my hand up. "And before you say it, my house isn't an option either. You know damn well they're staged out front ready to follow as soon as you leave the lot. Look what happened when we went to lunch the other day. They're just waiting for us to slip up. It's only a matter of time before they start chasing me, too."

As much as it pains me to say this, I think he

and I need to press pause on this whole thing. We were fine at first, had spent quite a few nights in each other's arms, but the more often we're seen together outside of the studio—no matter how innocent—the more aggressive the paparazzi becomes. They've even started hanging out in front of his house which sadly, put an end to our sleepovers.

Those assholes are determined to get their money shot proving Ethan and I are more than co-workers. Normally, they couldn't care less about celebrity chefs, but once they sniff a scandal, all bets are off. Look what happened to Martha and Paula.

He rolls his eyes. "We're on the same show, Gabs. We're allowed to be friendly. As far as they're concerned, we were discussing business. That's what I told Eric after he confronted me."

"That's exactly my point! If our producer is suspicious, he's going to be watching us now, too. I think maybe we need to table this...whatever this is between us, until after the last season wraps."

He lifts a brow. "You honestly think we can keep our hands off each other for the next three months?" My knees buckle when he leans over and trails his tongue down the nape of my neck. "I fucking want you all the time, Gabbie. Like I've never wanted anyone before. My willpower isn't that strong. I can do without the lunch dates, but I *need* you in my bed. We'll be more careful. I'll send a car to drive you to work tomorrow and you can come home with me afterwards. I'll take my Range Rover so you can hide in the back when we leave the studio. Nobody can see through those windows."

My head falls back when his mouth moves down to my cleavage. "What if they're still camped out at your house?"

I can feel his smile against my skin when I moan. "I'll park in the garage. They'll never know you're there. I need you, Gabs. I can't stop thinking about this beautiful body." He stands up straight and taps my temple. "And your mind. You're the most genuine person I've ever met in this town. How can you ask me to give that up?"

"Wait," I correct. "I'm asking you to *wait* until we finish filming. By then, we'll be released from our contracts so being seen together won't be an issue. Everyone will assume we fell for each other during the filming but we can't give the network proof that we did anything about it while under contract. It's too risky right now, no matter how many precautions we take. Too many people are watching us. Wait three months, then you can have me all you want."

He smirks. "*All* I want, *whenever* I want?"

I smile at his implication. "In *any position* you want."

Ethan groans. "You're killing me, woman."

I glance at the time. "I have to get on set. Wait a few minutes and then follow." I give him a light peck on the cheek before exiting my dressing room.

As I make my way down the hallway, I think to myself how the next few months of my life are going to seem like an eternity.

CHAPTER SEVEN

GABBIE

"It sounds like a warzone over there." My assistant, Caroline, rubs her temples. "God, my head is killing me."

I sigh. "They've gotta be almost done with renovations by now."

From the sounds of it, Ethan's new space is undergoing a major facelift. They have the windows blacked out, but Caroline and I have had to listen to construction noises through our rattling shared wall for over five weeks now. Sometimes it gets so loud, we have to shout to speak to our customers.

Caroline gives me a worried expression. "What's going to happen to us when they open?"

"Please," I scoff. "If anything, that asshole should be asking himself that question. We're one of the most recommended places in Santa Monica on TripAdvisor. People have been lining up around the corner since the day we opened. I don't know what he was thinking putting his new shop right next door."

I cringe internally at the blatant lie. I know without a doubt this is personal. What I don't know, is *why* Ethan feels I deserve any more torment. Didn't he put me through the wringer enough? And what in the hell did I do to deserve his wrath anyway? *He's* the one who wronged *me*!

My assistant scrubs the stainless steel work table aggressively. "Gabs, I need you to be honest with me. I can't afford my mortgage without this job. If you think I should start looking for a new position, I need time to find one."

I place a row of fresh berries over toasted crème fraîche, then turn around to face her. "Okay, look. I honestly don't know what's going to happen. Based on the popularity of his other stores, I can't imagine it will be good at first. But I have to believe that once the newness wears off, once people realize the *Baking Bad Boy* won't actually be manning the counter, they'll come back. Sweet Temptations is original. We have new items on rotation daily. *Better* items. You can't get that kind of authenticity with a chain."

"How do you know he won't be manning the counter?"

That's the one thing she focuses on?

I sigh. "Caroline, I know Ethan. And trust me when I say, that man thinks he's above serving the general public. He's either filming or gallivanting around with supermodels. If it doesn't involve lying on a beach or getting his face in front of a camera, he's not going to bother. The fact that we haven't seen said face around here since that first day is proof of that. Ethan will hire pastry chefs to follow his recipes and someone to manage the business side of it, but he won't be anywhere nearby. That's how he does it with the other two. Why would this location be any different?"

"I suppose time will tell." She looks around the kitchen. "Do you need me to do anything else before I take off?"

I wave her off. "Nah, I'll be fine. I just want to finish decorating this tart and then I'm out of here."

Caroline hangs her apron on the hook by the back door. "Okay, I'll see you bright and early then. Night, Gabs."

"Night." I close the door behind her and turn the lock.

Caroline must've forgotten her keys because no more than a minute later, the service door buzzer rings. I regret not looking at the security monitor when I open it and find the bane of my existence standing there with a smug smile.

I park a hand on my hip. "What do you want, Ethan? We're closed."

He barks out a laugh. "I'm aware. I've been waiting all damn day to get you alone. I thought your assistant would never leave."

I cock my head to the side. "You've been spying on me?"

Fine lines form on the outer corners of his baby blue eyes. Damn it, why does he have to get better looking with age?

"Less spying...more waiting for an opportunity to talk without an audience." He gestures behind me. "May I come in?"

I step aside. "Oh, why the hell not? What have I got to lose?"

When he crosses the threshold, his chest brushes against mine, despite the fact that he had plenty of room to avoid contact. I try to ignore the heat pooling between my thighs. Sadly, my nipples, obstinate bitches that they are, refuse to cooperate. I don't miss the way Ethan's gaze lingers on the peaked evidence of my arousal.

"It's cold in here," I mutter as I cross my arms over my chest.

He smirks. "If you're from Brazil, maybe." I flinch when he reaches out and swipes his thumb across my cheek. "You have a little something right here."

I make a conscious effort not to squirm when he

pops his thumb into his mouth and sucks the tangy filling from the tip. "It's lemon curd."

He gives me a dry look. "Obviously, I know that after tasting it. It's not bad. Not as good as mine, but not bad."

I roll my eyes at the backhanded compliment. "You said you wanted to talk, so talk."

"Right." Ethan's eyes slowly wander across my kitchen. He walks over to the wall where two eleven-rack convection ovens stand, running his hand over their double doors as if he were caressing a woman. "Nice setup you have here, Gabs. I'm impressed."

"Don't call me that," I snap.

"Call you what?"

"Gabs. Only people who haven't thrown me to the wolves have that right."

He whips around, the confusion evident in his expression. "What are you talking about?"

I slice my hand through the air dismissively. "It doesn't matter. Ancient history, right?"

Ethan's eyes narrow. "No. I think I'd like you to explain, *sweetheart*, considering you have it backwards."

What is he talking about?

I straighten my spine. "Save the endearments for your little Victoria's Secret model. Just say what you came here to say and get the hell out of my kitchen."

He smiles triumphantly. "Been keeping tabs on me, have you?"

"No," I sputter.

Ethan laughs. "Sure, you're not. But you might like to know that Ivanka and I weren't actually dating."

"Dating...fucking, whatever."

He takes a step toward me. "We weren't doing that either. It was a publicity thing. We're represented by the same firm. You should remember how that goes. Besides, she's not really my type."

"Right," I scoff. "Tall, blonde, and beautiful isn't your type?"

Ethan shakes his head slowly as he closes the gap between us. "I'm more into short, brunette, and *sexy-as-fuck*." I fight the urge to flee when he fingers a lock of hair that's escaped its bun.

He looks over my shoulder. "Isn't a lemon tart a bit generic?"

I narrow my eyes. "Not *that* lemon tart. Adding the toasted crème fraiche makes a *huge* difference. And the lemon curd is blended with mascarpone. It makes an ordinary tart *extraordinary*. I also ensure that the lemon is mild enough so it'll compliment whatever berries are in season."

Ethan lifts a brow in challenge. "May I?"

"Sure. I'm always open to giving lessons in humility." I grab a knife, aggressively cutting through the flaky crust. I lift the slice and turn toward him. "Here."

His eyes dance with amusement as he leans forward and takes a bite. As he chews, his gaze never leaves mine. Chewing isn't normally so sexy, but somehow when *he* chews, it is. Especially when his tongue snakes out to lick the cream off his lips.

He comes even closer, whispering against my ear. "I stand corrected. It's *exceptional*...just like the chef."

"Ethan, what are you doing?" I really hope that wasn't as breathy as it sounded in my head.

"I have no fucking idea." He nips my earlobe. "But I'm going to do it anyway."

Before I can even process his words, his lips are pressed against mine. Shocked, I gasp, which Ethan takes as his invitation to slip his tongue inside my mouth. I hear the pastry flop on my freshly mopped floor right before my nails dig into his firm biceps. I really should push him away but my hands loop behind his neck instead, pulling his body flush against mine.

Oh God, I forgot how well he can kiss.

He tastes like lemon and blueberries and sinful indulgence. My brain is telling me that I need to stop, but as his mouth moves against mine, my body begs for *more-more-more*. I've never met a man besides him that could drug me with a simple kiss. With a few strokes of his skilled tongue, I'm reduced to nothing but pure want.

Ethan pulls my hips roughly and effortlessly lifts my body onto the stainless-steel work surface behind me. I moan involuntarily as he spreads my thighs and grazes my clit through the thin fabric of my leggings.

"Fuck," he pants. "Why do you always have to feel so damn good?"

"Stop talking," I demand. "You'll ruin it."

What am I doing?

I despise this man. He threw me into a pit of vipers without any remorse. Yet, my body betrays me as my panties flood with arousal. When Ethan hums in approval, I know he can feel my wetness through my clothing. His thumb brushes back and forth over my sensitive nerves, the friction from the motion against my lace panties creating a delicious tension. It builds higher and higher until I'm on the verge of exploding.

Ethan releases a low growl before looping his fingers under the waistband of my pants, ripping them from my body in seconds, underwear and shoes included. I try not to think about how much practice he must've had at that to become so adept.

He slides his hands under my tunic, up my ribcage and over my breasts, brushing his knuckles against my taut nipples. Shamelessly, I push into his palms as he grips my breasts with an almost bruising force. This entire time, his icy stare remains fixated on me, watching my expression.

I lean forward and bite his lower lip. "This is stupid."

He returns the favor and pulls back with a smirk. "Don't fucking care."

In the next breath, Ethan drops to his knees, putting him at eye level with my exposed pussy. He yanks me forward, hooking my legs over his shoulders. I'm forced to lean back on my elbows so I don't hit my head against the table.

To my utter horror, I release a loud moan when his tongue snakes out, giving me one long lick down the center. I watch as his dark head of hair moves between my thighs, as he feasts on me like a man starved. It's the most erotic thing I've ever seen and my head falls back from the sheer ecstasy of what this man is doing to me.

"We're violating all sorts of health codes right now," I whimper.

Ethan pulls back slightly. "We'll bleach the shit out of it later."

I nod in agreement as he resumes his task of licking and sucking my hot flesh until my legs are squeezing his ears, until I'm screaming his name over and over. I can feel his smile against my skin as he trails soft kisses along my inner thigh. He stands with a devious grin and begins making quick work of undoing his black slacks. He lowers them just enough to free his cock and I have to stifle a gasp. My memory somehow blocked how impressive his erection is, likely so I wouldn't set unrealistic expectations with other men. Ethan hisses my name as I give him a hard squeeze before moving my fist up to the flared head, brushing my thumb over the precum leaking from the tip.

He pushes my hand away and his thumbs dig into my hips as he moves closer, burying himself to the root in one hard thrust. I can't even be ashamed of the needy mewl that rips from my throat because it feels too good when he slowly slides out and shoves himself back in again. I've only been with one other man since Ethan and that guy was nowhere near as well endowed. Nor skilled. It almost seems cruel that the one man I should stay far away from is the only one that can light my body on fire.

Without warning, Ethan withdraws, leaving me feeling unbearably empty. I'm about to question him but he beats me to the punch and shows me what he's doing instead. Just as easily as he propped me onto this table, he pulls me down and then turns me around so my back is pressed to his front. I slam my hands onto the cool surface as he thrusts into me once again. He flattens a palm between my shoulder blades, encouraging me to rest my chest against the table. I curl my fingers around the edges as Ethan sets an unyielding but oh-so-exquisite pace, giving me a good slap on the ass before rubbing the sting away. He's never been gentle with me because he knows I prefer sex with a slight edge to it. I never had to say a word either; this man could interpret my wants like no other. Sex has never been as good as it is with him.

"Fuck, Ethan, I'm so close."

I shiver as he fists my hair and bites my earlobe. "You want to come again, Gabbie? Beg a little and I'd be happy to oblige."

"Fuck you," I spit out.

He slams into me with a little extra force. "That's what I'm doing, sweetheart."

My jaw clenches. "Well, do it *better*."

Ethan pinches my clit, making my back bow in pleasure. "You've never *had better*, honey, and you fucking well know it."

I moan as he rolls my hot flesh between his fingers. "You give yourself too much credit."

His palm goes to where our bodies are joined. "Your dripping pussy says otherwise, Gabs."

"I told you not to call me that."

Ethan parts my ass cheeks and presses his now slicked finger against my tight hole. "I think I more than have that right when my dick is inside of you, *Gabs*."

I open my mouth to give him a snarky retort, but I wind up calling out his name instead as his finger presses forward at the same time he changes the angle of his dick. Warmth spreads down my spine when he hits that special spot inside of me, jerking me back into him. My whole body quakes as the force of my orgasm rushes over me, leaving me gasping for breath. When my spasms subside, Ethan moves inside of me with renewed purpose, until he's cursing into my neck and biting my shoulder as he finds his own release.

We stay there for a moment, practically bent in half, sweat sticking to the shirts we never got around to removing. The only sound in the room is our breath, slowly but surely returning to normal. Ethan hisses as he slides out of me. I don't move a muscle as I listen to him fastening his pants and belt. I hear what sounds like rustling paper so I crane my neck back to find the source. Sure enough, Ethan places a folded white square next to my outstretched arm.

I finger the corner of it. "What's this?"

"The reason I stopped by."

I stand up and turn around to face him. Thankfully, my shirt is long enough to cover my lady bits since I'm suddenly feeling too exposed. "I'm still on the pill, by the way. And clean. Thanks for asking."

Ethan's eyes widen, as if he's just now realizing we didn't use a condom. He clears his throat. "Me too. The clean part. I guess we got carried away."

I start unfolding the paper and mutter, "You can

say that again." My face warms as I look over the flier. "What the fuck, Ethan?"

He gives me a cocky smile. "Those are going out to the masses tomorrow. I thought you'd appreciate being the first person invited."

I scan the details of his grand opening invitation, scheduled for one week from tomorrow. "You asshole!" I shove his chest but he doesn't budge an inch. "Get the hell out of my bakery!"

The bastard holds his hands up in surrender as he backs away. "All right, all right, I'm going. Does that mean I can count on your attendance?"

"You can count on my knee hitting your balls if you don't get out of here in the next five seconds."

He actually has the nerve to laugh. "I see you're still a wildcat. Although, I already deduced that over the last thirty minutes."

My fists clench. "Go to hell!"

Ethan winks as he opens the back door. "I'll take that as a yes. See you next week, sweetheart."

I scream at the top of my lungs as the door slams behind him. I can't believe that son of a bitch just talked me out of my panties!

What have I done?

And what's the fallout going to look like this time?

CHAPTER EIGHT

ETHAN

"What do you mean you have a date tonight?"

Gabbie's eyes widen in warning, reminding me to lower my voice. "It's not a real date; my publicist arranged it. She wanted to drum up some buzz before season three premieres next week."

I clench my jaw. It's been almost two months since I've been able to lose myself in this woman so I'm a bit on edge. I know quite well how many dates are arranged strictly for publicity purposes—hell, I've been on a few this month alone to keep the media from sniffing around me and Gabbie—but I still don't like it. If anyone takes this woman out, it should be me.

"Who are they setting you up with?"

She takes my elbow and leads me into a dark corner of the set. We're rolling in less than five minutes so this probably isn't the best time to have this conversation but I'm not about to drop it after she gives me that sheepish look.

"Luke Warner."

"Are you fucking kidding me, Gabs?"

"Keep your voice down!" she whispers harshly. "We have the same agent and Luke's new show is airing next week as well. Plus, my publicist doesn't think we've quite dispelled all the rumors about us so this helps with that, too. It's a win-win."

I narrow my eyes. "You are *not* going out with Luke-fucking-Warner."

Gabbie looks around as the crew starts glancing our way. "It doesn't matter who it is. It's not real, Ethan."

"Don't think for a second that wasn't intentional," I grumble.

Luke Warner and I go way back. All the way to culinary school, in fact. And we've never gotten along well. Quite the opposite, actually. We've been pitted against each other competitively almost every step of the way in our climb to fame. Jobs, women, you name it, that man always goes after what I want. I have no doubt he set his eyes on Gabbie after the rumors about us started flying. This may not be a real date on her end, but I'd bet my Bugatti that he intends to make it one.

She sighs. "You're blowing this way out of proportion."

"Don't be an idiot, Gabriela. He wants to fuck you."

Gabbie glares at me. "Did you really just call me an idiot?"

I roll my eyes. "I said don't *be* an idiot. There's a difference."

She releases a sexy little growl. "You're unbelievable! And even if he *did* want in my pants, it wouldn't matter because I'm not interested. Give me a little credit, Ethan."

"Ethan! Gabbie!" our director, Jay, calls. "Places!"

I give her a stern look as I take the seat next to her at the judge's table. "This conversation isn't over."

Gabbie side-eyes me. "That's what you think."

CHAPTER NINE

NOW

GABBIE

"Gabriela Martinez?"

I look up as a slender blonde walks into the shop. She looks familiar but I can't quite place her.

"Yes, I'm Gabriela Martinez. How may I help you?"

"I'm Leslie Williams, a columnist from *Los Angeles News*. I was hoping we could talk for a few minutes."

That's where I know her from! She writes for the metro and entertainment section. She has a small picture and bio under each article she publishes. Caroline shoos me away, letting me know she can handle the line. I step from behind the counter to speak with the journalist.

I wipe my hands on my apron before shaking hers. "What can I do for you?"

She gives me a toothy smile. "I'm covering the grand opening for Baldwin's Bakery. I'd like to get a quote from you about it."

I bite my tongue to hold back my anger. "Why would you need a quote from me? I have no affiliation with them. You should be speaking with the owner."

Leslie's smile turns smarmy. "Miss Martinez, with all due respect, we both know you are well acquainted with the owner. I think our readers would like to know how you feel about Ethan Baldwin opening his new bakery *right next door* to your bakery. Surely you don't plan on staying here. Do you have plans to relocate Sweet Temptations?"

My jaw clenches so hard I have to make a conscious effort to loosen it so I can speak. "I have no comment."

She pouts. "Oh c'mon, woman to woman, I'm sure this isn't easy. After all of the drama from your past with him, this must sting. You really don't have *anything* to say?"

"Ms. Williams, with all due respect, I said I have *no comment*. Now, unless I can interest you in a pastry, I'll need to ask you to leave."

She brushes an imaginary piece of lint from her shoulder. "Well, thank you for your time. Perhaps I'll be able to convince Mr. Baldwin to comment on the matter."

I open the door for her and give her a fake smile. "Good luck with that. Have a great day!"

"You too, Miss Martinez."

Leslie flips her hair and gives me a cold look, in that bitchy way women do when they're sizing up their perceived competition. The joke's on her though, because if she wants Ethan, she can fucking have him. No matter how great he is in bed, he's an asshole through and through and I have no need for someone like that in my life. The other night was a mistake I have no intention of repeating.

CHAPTER TEN

ETHAN

"What in the hell are you doing?"

I lock the door behind me and continue advancing upon Gabbie until her ass hits the back wall of her dressing room.

"I said we weren't done with our conversation, Gabs. You can't just bolt to your dressing room and ignore me."

She throws her hands up. "And why not? There's nothing to discuss."

I press my body into hers and bite her earlobe. "That's bullshit. Tell your publicist to pick anyone *but* him. He's a prick."

Gabbie groans when I grind my erection against her. "He seemed perfectly nice on the phone."

"You talked to him on the phone?"

Her eyes narrow contemptuously. "Of course I

did. We needed to discuss when and where we're meeting. I have to be at The Ivy in an hour so I really need you to go so I can finish getting ready."

My hands slip under her dress, caressing her smooth skin.

Gabbie gasps when I give the thin string anchored to her shapely hips an experimental tug. "Ethan, what are you doing?"

I pull harder, creating a satisfying ripping sound right before the flimsy material falls to the ground. "Taking what's mine."

"Wha—"

She doesn't get a chance to finish because my lips are on hers in the next moment, demanding entry. Gabbie doesn't hesitate. She opens her mouth and welcomes me in, her desperation mirroring my own. My dick throbs against her stomach. Gabbie moans when I push two fingers inside of her, my thumb circling her clit.

She breaks away from my mouth. "Ethan. Get your dick inside of me. *Now.*"

I bite back a smile and quickly unfasten my pants. In one smooth motion, I'm lifting her up and thrusting inside of her. I groan and drop my head to her collarbone.

"Fuck, two months is way too long to go without this. You feel amazing, Gabs."

Amazing is an understatement. Nothing has ever felt better than being inside of this woman and something deep inside of me tells me that I will never get enough.

Gabbie locks her ankles behind my back and squeezes me with her thighs. "Move, Ethan. I don't have a lot of time."

I growl as I pull out almost completely and thrust back in. "Well, then I'm going to make damn sure you feel what *I* do to you while you're with *him*."

Her fists clench around my hair, holding on for dear life as I fuck her hard and fast against the wall. Gabbie bites my shoulder to muffle her screams. I do the same to hers to stifle my compulsion to shout her name. Our heavy breathing and the sound of skin slapping echoes throughout the room. The smell of sex clings to the air. Pure male satisfaction courses through me, knowing that Gabbie will be wearing our combined scent on her date tonight. Our dressing rooms aren't equipped with showers so she really has no choice.

My hands are squeezing her ass cheeks so hard, I'm certain she'll have bruises in the shape of my fingertips afterwards. She doesn't seem to mind though. In fact, the rougher I get during sex—the more primal—the more she gets off on it. Nothing overly kinky, but my girl *loves* a good, hard fuck. If I wasn't already convinced she was the perfect woman for me—someone I could easily spend the rest of my days with—that in itself would do the job.

Gabbie and I are compatible on every fucking level. I want the world to know that she's mine but if I have to temporarily hide my affection for her, then I'm going to make damn sure she knows who she belongs to. Maybe that makes me a Neanderthal, but quite frankly, I don't fucking care. This woman owns every part of me and I'd be a fool not to stake my own claim.

Her back arches when I change the angle a bit. "God, I missed this so much. I almost forgot how good it feels."

I grunt. "I could *never* forget how good this feels." I hold still inside of her and grab her chin so she's forced to look me in the eye. "I mean it, Gabs. I'm not good with saying those three little words, but that doesn't mean I don't feel it. Sex is different with you. *Everything* is different with you. *Better*. I think about you all the time and I want to be with you every second of the day. I don't want anyone *but* you. You've become a vital part of my life. You get what I'm saying?"

She nods quickly and places her palms against my cheeks. "I do. I feel the same."

I run my thumb along her lower lip. "I hate that you're going out with him."

Gabbie's face softens. "I know you do. And I'm sorry...I really am. But it's just like your outings with

Sienna Atwell. It takes the heat off of us until we can go public and it drums up publicity for the show. Strictly business." She leans forward and bites down on my lower lip, making my cock twitch. "Would it help if I said I'll be thinking of you the entire time?"

I smile. "Maybe. It'd be even better if you told me that my dick is magical." I start moving again, slowly building up speed.

She gasps. "So fucking magical."

"Now that we have that settled..." I nip the side of her neck. "Hold on, baby. I'm going to make you come harder than you ever have before."

Gabbie looks me dead in the eye, the challenge unmistakable. "Bring it, Baldwin."

CHAPTER ELEVEN

NOW

GABBIE

Three.

That's exactly how many people came through my door today. And that's two more than yesterday. In the month since Baldwin's Bakery opened, I think it's safe to say they're doing well. And much to my surprise, Ethan has been running the place himself—according to the feature I read online anyway. I tried staying away from the window, but curiosity got the best of me after the third day and I saw quite a few of my regulars standing in line waiting to enter Ethan's store. I'm not going to lie; it hurt. A lot.

With a sigh, Caroline places the last box in her car. "Okay, I'm going to drop these off and then head home."

I glance at the dozen or so boxes stacked carefully in her trunk. Before Baldwin's opened, I couldn't tell you when the last time was that I had any product left over, but here I am, with almost two hundred unsold pastries for the twentieth day in a row. Since they don't have any preservatives, donating them to the homeless shelter is my only chance of ensuring they'll get eaten before they go bad. At least some good will come out of this, I suppose.

"Thanks for doing that, Care."

She closes the trunk. "Of course. I'll see you in the morning then?"

I nod. "I think we need to back off on production, at least until things pick up again. I can handle everything in the morning if you want to sleep in. Maybe come in around ten?"

Caroline gives me a sad smile. "Sure. I'll see you at ten."

I watch Caroline drive away before sliding into my car. I put the key in the ignition but I can't seem to gather the strength to crank the engine. I think the last few weeks are finally catching up to me. I feel fucking clobbered. I rest my head on the steering wheel, close my eyes, and take a few deep breaths to center myself. Despite my best efforts, tears start pouring down my face.

I knew business would suffer initially when Ethan opened his doors but I honestly didn't expect it to be *this* bad. I never thought my regulars would be lured by the flashiness of a new store. I've established relationships with them. I know them by name and what they like to order. I feel like a fool for having believed that would be enough.

I don't know how long I've been sitting here crying, but I think it's been a while when there's a knock on my driver's side window. I jump in my seat and look up to find the bastard responsible for my problem. I quickly wipe away my tears and try gathering my wits. I turn my key and roll down my window.

"I'm not in the mood to listen to any gloating, Ethan."

He frowns and actually has the nerve to look contrite. "Are you okay?"

I belt out a humorless laugh, which if I'm being honest, sounds a bit hysterical. "Yeah, just great."

I try rolling up my window but his hand stops its progress. "Wait, Gabbie. I'm serious. Are you okay?"

I roll my eyes. "Don't pretend that you care, Ethan. You should be happy. It looks like your plan's working. My business—my fucking livelihood —is tanking. If this keeps up, I'm not sure how much longer I can stay afloat. Is that what you wanted to hear? Does that make you fucking happy? I don't know why you felt the need to screw me over more than you already had, but what's done is done. As long as you're happy, that's all that matters, right?"

He shakes his head. "I..." He runs a hand through his hair and tries again. "That's not all that matters."

I scoff. "Yeah, well, actions speak louder than words. Goodbye, Ethan."

I shift my car into drive and pull away right before bursting into tears again.

CHAPTER TWELVE

NOW

ETHAN

As I watch Gabbie drive away, I feel sick. It fucking kills me seeing her cry—knowing I'm the cause of her sadness. That's ridiculous, right? This woman stomped all over my heart with no regret, yet watching her break down in her car, when she thought no one was watching, tore me apart. I was running purely on instinct when I approached her, intending to take her into my arms, and never let go. And then she spoke, throwing me completely off guard with her comment that I'd screwed her over back then. That's the second time she's alluded to me being at fault for the demise of our relationship, which confuses the hell out of me.

She has to be fucking with me; it must be all part of the sick games she likes to play. But as I recall the look on her face as she said it—how devastated she seemed to be—I don't think even the best actress in the world could fake that. So, again, I'm back to being clueless about what the fuck is happening. I should be stoked her business is failing, that my revenge is coming into fruition, but instead, I just feel like an asshole.

CHAPTER THIRTEEN

THEN

GABBIE

"I had a nice time tonight, Luke. Thank you."

"Me too." He smiles. "I've gotta say, this is the best PR setup I've ever had."

I chuckle. "This is the *only* PR setup I've ever had, so I don't really have anything to compare it to. But I did enjoy myself."

"So, maybe we should do this again. For real."

"Oh. Um..." I dig my keys out of my purse, trying to figure out what to say without revealing my relationship with Ethan.

Luke pushes a strand of hair behind my ear. "Gabbie, look at me."

I tilt my chin up to meet his eyes but the second I do his lips are pressed against mine. The kiss only lasts for a few seconds, and there's no tongue involved, but I'm instantly flooded with guilt. I know people have different levels of cheating, but in my opinion, a kiss is just as intimate as having sex if you're committed to someone else.

I pull back and blink a few times. "Luke...I, uh...I'm actually seeing someone. I'm sorry, but we're exclusive."

I think. Ethan and I haven't really had *the talk*, but it's been implied.

Luke raises an eyebrow. "Baldwin?"

I bite my lip. "I'd rather not say his name. We're keeping it quiet for now."

He smirks. "So, that's a yes."

My eyes widen. "I didn't—"

Luke laughs and grabs my hand, placing a soft kiss on my knuckles. "Relax, Gabbie, I won't say anything, other than he's a lucky bastard." He squeezes my hand. "How about this? I really did enjoy spending time together tonight. So, what if we try being friends? We obviously get along and have things in common. What harm could it do?"

"Uh..."

He gives me a boyish grin. "Yeah, I know Baldwin can't stand me, but I'm not asking to be friends with *him* and I have no interest in pursuing a woman who's already taken. I've done some things in my life that I regret but that was *never* one of them. What do you say? Can I at least keep your number on standby?"

I suppose that wouldn't hurt. I really do think

he's a nice guy, and he's right; we do have a lot in common. I know this is strange considering we just met, but I'm comfortable with him, like he's an old friend. I'm smart enough to know how rare that is.

"Okay, I think that would be all right."

"Okay, then." He opens his arms. "Should we hug it out?"

I chuckle. "Sure."

Luke pulls me into his arms and gives me a quick hug. When we're done, he opens the storm door and gestures for me to unlock my front door. As soon as it's opened, he steps backwards off the porch and gives me an adorable little salute.

"It's been a pleasure, Gabbie. Until next time."

I wave. "Until next time."

As I step inside, I wonder how in the hell Ethan is going to handle the prospect of me being friends with his nemesis.

CHAPTER FOURTEEN

ETHAN

I'm woken from a hot as fuck dream about Gabbie by my publicist's ringtone. I check the time before hitting the button to accept the call.

"Avery, why are you calling me in the middle of the night?"

"Where are you, Ethan?"

I sit up and rub the back of my neck. If Avery Jacobs-Maxwell is calling me at three in the morning with that tone, I'm not going to like what she has to say.

"I'm at home. Why?"

"Alone?" she counters.

"Yes, alone. What's going on, Ave?"

"Get to Ken's office ASAP. And whatever you do, do *not* look at the internet."

I pull the phone away from my ear for a second. "What the hell is going on?"

She sighs. "I'll explain everything at your agent's office. Do not make any stops or talk to anyone on the way. We need to do some major damage control and I don't need you fucking that up. Understand?"

I hang up the phone and stumble into my walk-in closet to get dressed. Avery is one of the best publicists in Hollywood. I'm lucky as hell to have her, but she can be a real ballbuster sometimes.

When I get to the automatic gates at the end of my driveway, the damn paparazzi has tripled in size. They're trying desperately to get my attention, flashes blinding me as I drive past them. It takes me about twenty minutes to get downtown to my agent's office. Cameramen are staged in front of his building as well, but thankfully, the parking garage is private, only accessible with a code.

Seriously, what the fuck is going on?

I take the elevator to the tenth floor, and walk straight into Ken Brighton's office. He's wearing wrinkled flannel pajamas and looks tired as fuck. Apparently, I'm not the only one Avery got out of bed.

My publicist of course, looks as well coiffed as she always does. Designer suit, red-soled heels, and not a hair out of place. Her arms are crossed as she stares me down, telling me she means business.

"Take a seat, Ethan."

I resist the urge to roll my eyes as I take a seat in front of Ken's desk. I'm a grown ass man yet this woman has a way of making me feel like I've been sent to the principal's office.

At Avery's prompting, Ken pushes a few buttons on his laptop and turns the monitor toward me. It takes me a moment to piece together what I'm looking at, but the second it hits me, I slam the computer shut and bolt out of my chair.

"What the fuck is that?" I'm pointing at Ken's MacBook like it's offended me greatly, which essentially, it has.

Avery taps her foot. "You're officially an amateur porn star now. This is all over the internet."

My mouth gapes. It's not often I find myself speechless but I couldn't piece together a sentence right now to save my life. My brain is too busy flashing high-def images of me fucking Gabbie against the wall in her dressing room. Thankfully, we were both almost completely clothed, with the exception of my ass hanging out, but with the clarity and the angle, there's absolutely no way to deny that we're the two people in that video. Or what we're doing.

Avery waits me out and after a minute or so, I finally find my voice. "How in the hell did they get this? You've got to get them to take it down, Avery!"

She shakes her head. "I've already sent cease and desist orders, Ethan. Give me some fucking credit. The problem is that, as you know, once something's on the internet, it's never truly gone." She picks up a manila folder off Ken's desk and removes a stack of photos, laying them out across the wooden surface. "In addition to the video, these are out there."

I assess each picture, getting more irate by the second. It's a series of shots taken of Gabbie and Luke Warner, clearly from last night because she's wearing the same dress. Every one of them depicts some act of intimacy. He's cradling her face, holding her in his arms, kissing her fucking *lips*.

"What is this shit?" I roar.

Ken raises his hands in a placating gesture. "Ethan, calm down."

I kick the fucking chair across the room. "How the hell am I supposed to calm down? One of you needs to explain what's happening before I drive to that fucker's house and knock his pretty boy teeth out."

"That's the last thing you will do!" Avery shouts. "Now, sit the hell down and I will explain."

I turn the chair upright and sit down. "Make it fast, Avery. My patience is pretty much nonexistent right now."

I'll give her this. I'm a big guy, and while I'd *never* hurt a woman, I must look scary as hell right now. At maybe five-foot-two, Avery is *tiny* and she looks ready to go a few rounds with me, not intimidated in the least.

Avery takes the seat beside me. "In short, you've been played."

My jaw tics. "Care to elaborate?"

"Look, Ethan, I know you like her, but Gabriela Martinez is behind all of this. Considering your history with Warner, I'd say they planned this together."

"There's no fucking way," I scoff. "And I more than fucking like her, Ave. *I'm in goddamn love with her!*"

Sympathy crosses her face. "Ethan, listen to me. I got ahold of the pap that sold these pictures. He flat out admitted that she set up a hidden camera in her dressing room and gave the footage to him."

I shake my head in disbelief. "Why would she do that? She's under contract, too. And it's not like I *planned* on fucking her in there. We've *never* had sex in her dressing room before last night. It was completely spontaneous. And she just met Warner yesterday!"

She lifts a perfectly sculpted brow. "Are you sure about that?" Avery fingers the corner of the photo where Luke is kissing my girl. "Don't you think it's possible you've been set up? Look at these pictures, Ethan. There's familiarity between them. This does not look like two people who just met, which is exactly how the gossip rags are spinning it. They've made a fool out of you."

I fold my arms across my chest. "Again, Gabbie could be sued for breach of contract just the same as I can. Why in the fuck would she risk that?"

She shrugs. "My best guess is that she's trying to get her fifteen minutes of fame."

"She's already famous!"

Avery shakes her head. "Hardly. And my sources tell me she's being offered another position at the Food Channel, so burning bridges with the Cooking Network isn't an issue for her. As for any potential lawsuits, the network just says that to scare you. I've already spoken with them and they're modifying your contracts to remove the clause so they don't lose any more sponsors.

"With your ratings being so high, they're not going to pull the last season right before it goes live. Plus, we're all fairly certain this scandal will make the numbers go through the roof. The world will be watching, just waiting for the drama to unfold between the judges."

"This is bullshit! I need to talk to Gabbie. She'll clear this up."

Ken shakes his head. "You can't do that, Ethan. The pap is willing to go on record saying she was the source. If you're linked with her right now, in any way, you're fucked. Let Avery do her job. She's going to spin this to make Gabriela look like the fame whore she is, and you'll look like the guy who had his heart broken. The public will be eating out of your hands and Gabriela's career will be flushed down the drain."

"You can't vilify her," I insist.

"And why the hell not?" Avery throws her hands up. "She *is* the villain in this! She and Luke Warner fucked you over. How can you not want justice for that?"

I pull my phone out of my pocket and scroll through my contacts. "I'm calling her."

Avery's arm lashes out like a viper and snatches the phone away from me. "No. You won't. Listen to me very carefully, Ethan. If you want to come out of this with your reputation and career intact, you will let me handle this. I've already reached out to her PR team. As of right now, they have no comment. That's very telling, don't you think? If she was innocent, they'd want to work *with* me to clear this up."

"Give me my fucking phone back, Avery. You can't tell me what to do."

She raises her eyebrows. "It's *my job* to tell you what to do when you're in deep shit like this, Ethan. And if you can't follow my directions to clean this up, I'll drop you as my client faster than you can blink. Then where will you be? You know we need to take action immediately. You know I'm your best hope. Just let me deal with it and, whatever you do, do *not* talk to Gabriela Martinez." She scrolls through my phone and punches the screen a few times. "There. She's blocked from calling you."

"Not talking to her will be rather hard when we still have a month's left of filming."

Avery and Ken share a look before she turns back to me and sighs. "I'm dead serious, Ethan. Think with the right head here. The *only* time you talk to her is when you're filming. The second the director yells cut, your lips are sealed. You got it?"

"Yeah, I fucking got it," I mutter.

CHAPTER FIFTEEN

NOW

GABBIE

Great, this is exactly what I don't need right now.

As I pull into my parking spot behind Sweet Temptations, I see Ethan leaning against my back door, blocking my entry. I could let myself in through the front but knowing Ethan, he'd follow me. He'd obviously like to continue our conversation from last night, which is the absolute last thing I want to do at five in the morning.

I barely slept and my head is killing me from crying for hours on end. I was already dreading another slow day. Starting it off with a reminder of why I'm in this predicament in the first place, is just about the worst way to launch into the workday.

I take a deep breath and get out of my car, ready to face the firing squad.

When I reach the door, I jingle my keys, gesturing for him to step aside. "Could you move, please? I need to get to work."

Ethan steps aside, but only marginally. "Go right ahead."

I freeze as I insert the key into the lock. Ethan's large frame is pressed against my back. I can feel every muscle in his body and if I'm not mistaken, his growing erection. Oh, who am I kidding? Unless he has a cucumber stuffed in his pocket, I know exactly what that is. I have to suppress a shiver when he presses his lips against my ear.

"We need to talk, Gabbie."

I squeeze my eyes shut and bite my tongue, hoping the sharp pain will snap me out of my lust-induced stupor. I hate that despite everything that's happened between us, my body still responds to him like this.

I open the door with so much force, I practically smack myself in the face with it. "We have nothing to talk about, Ethan. Don't you need to get inside your own bakery? I'm sure you have quite the work-load to prepare for all your customers."

He completely ignores my snarky comment and follows me inside, waiting as I disarm the alarm system. He locks the door behind him and casually leans against the wall beside it.

I need coffee for this shit.

I walk to the front without a word, fire up the

espresso machine, and take my sweet time making a latte. My *mamá's* voice is screaming inside my head to mind my manners and offer my guest a drink, but I ignore it. The less comfortable he is, the sooner he'll leave.

I hope.

Ethan rests his shoulder in the small doorway connected to the kitchen, watching me in complete silence.

I set my cup on the counter. "Oh, for fuck's sake! What, Ethan? What could you possibly want?"

The bastard smirks. "Glad to see the fire's back. I much prefer this to the crying."

I glare. "Get to the point."

He takes a step forward. "Gab—"

I hold my hand up. "Stay right there. I can't think when you're within touching distance."

He stays in the same spot but his bright blue eyes roam over my body so thoroughly, I can practically feel his hands dancing over my skin. Damn it, I need to get him out of here.

I raise my eyebrows. "Well?"

Ethan clears his throat. "I need you to explain what you meant about me screwing you over."

"Why? You were there. You know exactly what happened."

He shakes his head. "Here's the problem with that: I *thought* I knew what happened. But now, I'm not so sure. Things aren't adding up, Gabbie. I think I need to hear it directly from you. I'm two years too fucking late in asking, but I need to get your perspective."

I sigh. "What will that accomplish? What's done is done. I really don't want to relive the past. That period in time wasn't exactly fun for me."

His spine stiffens. "You think it was fun for me? Seeing you with him fucking crushed me!"

"Luke and I were just friends!" I shout back.

Ethan scoffs. "Fucking friends. Right. It didn't look that way to me. If you two were supposedly *just friends*, one would think you'd try mitigating the rumors. Spending every waking moment together does the opposite. *Kissing him* does the opposite!"

My fists clench. "Well, it's the truth! While I was being crucified by the media—for no reason whatso-ever—he was there for me! We didn't spend every waking moment together, but you of all people should know how the media likes to sensationalize things. As for the kissing, Luke and I didn't get involved until six months after shit hit the fan. What was I supposed to do, Ethan? I know how bad it looked, but you couldn't even afford me the courtesy of explaining my side of the story. You just automati-cally assumed the worst and completely wrote me off.

"You made me feel loved one minute and in the next, you treated me like dog shit stuck on the bottom of your shoe! It doesn't matter what the truth is anymore. The fact that you thought I was capable of doing something so heinous tells me all I need to know. You think you were crushed? If any part of you was actually crushed, it was your goddamn ego. You'd have to actually love someone to have your heart broken."

His eyes are lit with fire. "You think I didn't love you?"

I laugh humorlessly. "I know you didn't."

Ethan's nostrils flare. "Fuck that." His long legs eat up the space between us and before I know it, he's kissing me. I'm ashamed to admit it, but I link my fingers behind his neck and kiss him back with everything I have.

He pulls back, biting my lip as he goes, and rests his forehead against mine. "Does that feel like I didn't love you? That I don't *still* love you?"

What am I doing? I can't fall into this trap again. I barely survived the first time.

I press my open palms against his chest, pushing him away. "Please leave, Ethan."

He straightens to his full height. "You want me to leave? Right now?"

I blink back the tears that are threatening to fall. "Yes. And I don't want you to come back. I don't know how much longer I'll be able to stay here, but as long as we're neighbors, I'd appreciate it if you would pretend we weren't. Better yet, pretend that we never met."

Ethan shakes his head. "I can't do that, Gabbie."

I unlock the front door and hold it open. "Please go."

He steps toward the exit but stops over the threshold. "I'll leave, because I need to sort through some shit, but I'm not going anywhere. You get what I'm saying?"

I have to bite my tongue to avoid responding. Instead, my eyes flash to the sidewalk, silently dismissing him. The moment he steps outside, I lock the door but make the mistake of looking up. Ethan's eyes are boring into mine from the other side of the glass, as if searching for something. I manage to hold his stare for only a few seconds before I run to the back so he can't see me cry again.

CHAPTER SIXTEEN

GABBIE

"What is going on, Margo? The paparazzi are surrounding my house!"

Over the phone line, my publicist sighs. "I take it you haven't spoken with Ethan Baldwin yet?"

I shake my head but then realize she can't see me. "No. I tried calling him as soon as I saw the photographers out front but something's wrong with his phone. I keep getting a recorded message saying my call can't go through."

"They've probably blocked your number. Listen, the official statement we have out right now is, 'no comment'. I wanted to get your side of it before I said anything else."

"No comment about *what?* I don't understand what's happening right now."

I can hear her fingers tapping along a keyboard.

"You were followed on your date last night. Which would've been fine, if the video hadn't been leaked."

I pace in circles around my living room and peek through the curtains to see if the photographers are gone yet. No such luck. "What video? What are you talking about?"

"Check your email, Gabbie. I just sent you something."

"Hold on a sec."

I switch my phone to speaker and open my inbox. Holy shit, I have over two hundred new messages, mostly from addresses I don't recognize. What the hell? I click on the email from my **PR** firm and open the attachment. I gasp in shock the moment it starts playing. On my screen is a crystal-clear video of me and Ethan having sex last night. Where did this come from? And how did my publicist get it?

"Wha...what is this, Margo?"

"Gabriela, I need you to be honest with me or I can't do my job. Is that you and Ethan Baldwin in that video?"

"Yes...but I don't understand. We weren't filming ourselves. Where did you get this?"

She sighs even louder this time. I swear I just heard her thunk her head against a hard surface. "Click on the link I sent you."

I'm taken to *Celebrity Gossip Central,* the internet's

leading tabloid website. At the top of the page in bold red print are the words, *"Baking Masters Judges Caught With Their Pants Down."* Below that is a pixelated version of the video, blocking out Ethan's ass but showing everything else. Farther down the page, they have a sequence of pictures from my date with Luke Warner.

Those slimy bastards.

With just the right angle, they managed to make a purely innocent moment look salacious. Well, except for the very brief kiss we had, but even that looks much worse than it was. From this, it looks like we were making out.

I quickly read through the article that accuses me of having affairs with both men. It suggests that I may have seduced Ethan away from his ex-girlfriend, an A-list actress named Natasha. It speculates that I was using both Ethan and Luke to elevate my own fame and secure a more lucrative contract with the Food Channel. They conveniently failed to mention that I turned down that network's offer.

"What the fuck?" I shout when I get to the statement from Ethan's publicist.

Ethan Baldwin was under the impression that he was in a monogamous relationship with Ms. Martinez, a woman whom he loves deeply. These photos clearly indicate that the exclusivity was on his end only. I assure you he did not begin his relationship with Ms. Martinez while still attached to Natasha Kozlov. Mr. Baldwin is understandably upset; therefore, we ask that you respect his privacy during this difficult time.

The article concludes by stating that there is no comment from me, Luke, or the network at this time.

I'm so angry I'm shaking. I have to sit down on my couch and set the phone on the coffee table in front of me.

"How did this happen, Margo? What do we do now?"

"Gabbie, the man who sold the video went on record saying that he received the footage from you."

"What?!"

"Are you saying that isn't accurate?"

"Of course that isn't accurate! I don't even know how someone could've set up a camera in my dressing room!"

"The studio has postponed production for the day. The producers are demanding a meeting with both you and Ethan. They've agreed to remove the no fraternization clause in your contracts but they want to discuss things with you first. I've already called your agent and lawyer and they'll be there to represent you, just in case."

"Then what?"

"Then, we go from there, depending on what

they say. As you know, I also represent Luke so I'm sure you can imagine how many things I have on my plate right now. I'm meeting with him in an hour to discuss what we'd like his official statement to be. I'll meet with you to do the same as soon as your meeting lets out. For now, head to network's corporate building downtown, and do not speak to anyone unless it's someone from the show or your team. Understand?"

I hang my head in my hands. "Do I have a choice?"

"Not really."

I nod. "I guess I'll see you in a bit."

"See you then, Gabs. We'll get this figured out."

I fight back tears as I press the end button. I don't see how we can fix this after Ethan's publicist's statement. Why would she do that? I guess the only way I'm going to find out is by asking the man himself.

CHAPTER SEVENTEEN

NOW

ETHAN

"I need you to track down the guy who sold my sex tape."

"Why would I do that?" I can practically see my publicist rolling her eyes through the phone.

"Because, I want the name of the person that really gave the footage to him. Whatever they paid him, I'll pay more for the truth once he goes on record with it."

Avery laughs. "You can't be serious, Ethan. Why would you even want to stir this up again?"

Because my gut is telling me that I'm destroying a woman who doesn't deserve it.

I scrub a hand over my face. "I don't think she did it."

"Damn it, Ethan. This is your dick talking. I told you not to open your store by the pier. I told you to stay far away from Gabriela Martinez. Why couldn't you just listen?"

"Avery, I know you know your shit, but something's not right. If I was thinking rationally back then, I probably would've fought you harder on it. Gabbie was the best thing that ever happened to me and I threw her away like she meant nothing. Seeing her again, now that I can look at the situation logically, I know I fucked up by letting her go. I don't have proof yet, but I fucking *know* it."

She sighs. "Fine. I'll make some calls."

I smile. "Let me know."

"Yeah, yeah," she mutters before ending the call.

While she's doing that, I need to make some calls of my own. One way or the other, I'm going to make this right.

CHAPTER EIGHTEEN

GABBIE

"Miss Martinez, please have a seat," our producer, Eric, says as I knock on the open doorframe.

I walk into the conference room, evidently the last one to arrive. The long mahogany table is filled with people. Network executives, our producer, director, my agent and lawyer, and finally, Ethan and his team. I stifle a gasp when we make eye contact. His cold glare feels like a slap across the face. The tension radiating between us is tangible. I open my mouth to greet him, but my attorney, Jeff, interrupts and steps between us.

"Gabbie, come sit by me." He leans down and lowers his voice. "Do *not* say a word unless I give you permission."

"Did Margo call you?" I whisper back.

"Yes," Jeff says harshly. "I know where you stand. Now let me do the talking."

I lower myself into the chair as our producer says, "Thank you for coming to this meeting with so little notice. As we're all aware, we have yet another scandal on our hands, and I'd like to manage the situation with as little collateral damage as possible."

I avert my eyes to the polished tabletop, feeling my cheeks flush at the realization that every person in this room has likely seen that video. *Seen me having sex.* Thank God there wasn't any nudity on my end, but still, it's obvious that Ethan's dick was inside of me. I groan inwardly, wondering what these people must think of me right now.

"So..." Eric continues, "after speaking with Mr. Baldwin's and Ms. Martinez's representatives, I feel confident we have a solid plan."

My lawyer slides a document in front of me and hands me a pen from the breast pocket of his suit jacket. I look it over as our producer keeps talking.

"Since both parties have confirmed that the...*incident* in question was consensual, the network has agreed to remove the no fraternization clause from their contracts. That said, it's contingent upon both parties agreeing to film the rest of their contracted segments without regard to their personal relationship." Eric looks in my direction. "Or lack thereof."

What?

Eric clears his throat. "When the cameras are rolling, they will smile and act friendly toward one another. Additionally, since we've already lost several sponsors, both parties agree to take a significant pay cut to compensate for that. In return, the network will not pursue any legal action toward them for breaching their contracts."

I immediately glance at Ethan and find his gaze directed toward the front of the room, pointedly ignoring me. His nostrils flare, as if he's angry. Does he actually think I'm guilty?

Our producer pinches the bridge of his nose. "Furthermore, the network has decided to table any future opportunities within the Cooking Network for both parties. We will reevaluate that after they fulfill their current obligation. Any questions?"

Yeah, I have a shit ton of questions but none that I'm going to ask in front of an audience.

Eric's eyes slide to mine and then Ethan's. "If you agree to the terms, I need you to sign the amendment in front of you."

Ethan signs so forcefully, I swear he almost poked a hole through the paper.

My lawyer taps his finger on the signature line. "Sign it, Gabriela. This is the best possible outcome we have."

I don't know about that, but I sign anyway after reading through the final paragraph.

Eric nods, apparently satisfied that we've signed.

After several people shake their heads our producer nods. "Very well. Thank you for coming today. We'll resume filming as scheduled at seven tomorrow morning."

The network suits leave the room while I'm still sitting in my chair, trying to digest what's just happened. I practically leap out of my seat as soon as I spot Ethan trying to make a quick exit.

His muscles tighten when I grab his forearm. "Wait, Ethan. Can we talk?" I look around. "Privately?"

Ethan jerks his arm away from me and glances at his lawyer, a fifty-something woman with a fierce expression. "Ms. Martinez, Mr. Baldwin has requested that you limit your conversations with him to those required when filming. Beyond that, he has no desire to speak with you."

My mouth gapes. "What? You can't be serious." I turn toward Ethan. "You don't think I actually did this, do you?" Ethan looks me over with so much disgust, his answer is obvious. "Oh my God, you do! What the hell, Ethan?"

His agent—Ken something, I believe—leads him out of the room. "Let's go, Ethan."

I stand in the doorway, completely dumbstruck as Ethan and his entourage walk away without a backwards glance.

My agent, Barb, takes me by the elbow.

"C'mon, Gabbie, let's grab some coffee. Margo is meeting us at the Starbucks on the corner. After we gather a formal statement, we'll discuss how we'll handle your future with the network."

"I don't want a future with the network." I shake my head as I wipe a rogue tear from my cheek. "I'm done."

"That's not necessarily true," Barb counters. "If your third season ratings are as strong as we suspect, I'm sure they'll want to renew."

I sniff and look her in the eye. "You're not getting it, Barb. I'm *done*, done. I want out of the public eye if this is what it's like. After this season is over, I want *nothing* to do with this world."

She sighs. "Gabbie, I know this is hard, but it's a minor speedbump in the grand scheme of things. Don't be rash."

I laugh humorlessly. "Maybe it's minor to you because you see this kind of thing all the time, but it's not minor *in any way* to me. The world has seen me having sex! They think I'm a fame monger! No matter what I say, after Ethan's statement and the pictures online, no one will believe me. I don't need to meet with Margo. My official statement is *no comment.*"

Barb blinks rapidly. "I'm not your publicist, but I think that would be a big mistake, Gabbie. Let's go talk to Margo and we'll get this to blow over soon enough."

I furiously swipe at the tears that are now flowing freely. "I appreciate all that you've done for me, but I mean it. I'm done. This is not what I signed up for. I won't be needing your services or Margo's after today. Goodbye, Barb."

As I drive away from the Cooking Network's building, I think about what lies ahead. If Ethan's not even willing to listen to what I have to say, then I obviously didn't mean as much to him as I thought. I don't know how I'm going to sit next to him for twelve hours a day over the next month and pretend everything's okay, but I'm going to have to figure it out.

CHAPTER NINETEEN

NOW

ETHAN

"Are you sure about this, Ethan?" my realtor, Hank, asks.

"I'm positive," I say. "Get the paperwork ready and I'll take care of the rest."

I end the call and dial the woman who manages my finances next.

She picks up on the first ring. "Hello, little brother. To what do I owe the pleasure of this call?"

I decide to get straight to the point. "Hey, Liz. I'm closing the new store, effective immediately."

"What?" my sister asks incredulously. "You've barely been open a month and sales are through the roof. Why would you even think about closing now?"

"Because I fucked up and I need to make things right."

"Is this about a certain Latina next door?"

Jesus, I can practically see the condescending smirk on her face. When everything went down with Gabbie, Elizabeth tried convincing me to talk it through with her, to hear her side of the story, but I refused. I'm sure Liz is dying to shout, "I told you so!" right now.

"Maybe."

"I'm proud of you for finally pulling your head out of your ass, Ethan. Even though it's going to cost you a small fortune to dig yourself out of this."

I wave my hand dismissively. "I don't care about the money. This is more important."

"So...what's the plan? Are you selling and relocating?"

"Neither. I'm just closing up shop. Don't worry; I'll give the existing staff a nice severance package plus another opportunity for work again soon."

Liz clears her throat. "Ethan, I'm behind you one-hundred-percent, but as your financial advisor, I'm professionally obligated to tell you what a mistake that would be. That's valuable real estate. At the very least, put the property back on the market or consider leasing it."

"Can't," I say. "I already have plans for it."

"What are you not telling me?"

I smile. "You'll find out soon enough."

GABBIE

"Not that I'm complaining, but what the hell's happening today?" Caroline asks.

I smile. "Maybe people are finally coming to their senses."

Sweet Temptations has been swamped since we opened the doors. It's just after ten in the morning and we're already low on inventory. I had to call in a few of my part-timers to work the register so Caroline and I could head in the back and throw some more stuff in the oven. My head's been all messed up since my encounter with Ethan yesterday but we've been so busy today, I haven't had much chance to dwell on it.

As I'm placing a colorful tray of macarons in the display case, I'm shocked by what I overhear.

"Do you know why they closed so suddenly?"

"No," my employee, Denise, says. "I didn't even know about it until you said something. It explains why we've been so busy though."

I stand upright. "Who closed?"

The customer nods to her left. "Baldwin's Bakery. There's a sign on the store saying they're closed indefinitely."

What?

This is something I have to see for myself. I step from behind the counter and head through the front door. Sure enough, there's a handwritten sign on Ethan's front door.

Baldwin's Bakery is no longer operating at this location.
Sweet Temptations has the best confections in town.
Step next door and see for yourself!

I close my eyes to clear my vision. Surely, I'm seeing things. When I reopen them, the sign hasn't changed.

What is going on?

"Uh, Gabbie, could you step back into the kitchen please?"

I look up at the sound of Caroline's voice and see her poking her head out the front door. "Sure. Of course." I weave my way through the line of customers on the way back in, muttering, "excuse me," as I pass them.

I stop mid-stride when I see Ethan standing in my kitchen donning his signature black apron.

"What is *he* doing here?" I look to Caroline for answers but she simply smiles and busies herself with a piping bag.

Traitor!

"You look like you could use some help." Ethan spreads his arms wide. "Put me to work, Gabs."

I don't mean to stare, but c'mon! I'm pretty sure I'm hallucinating right now.

He clears his throat. "Did you hear what I said?"

I blink repeatedly. "I did. But I'm still trying to figure out whether or not you're a mirage."

Ethan belts out a husky laugh. "You're more than welcome to touch me and find out. Go ahead and run your hands *all* over my body. I'm sure you'll enjoy it almost as much as I will."

I roll my eyes and fight a smile, reminding myself what this man has put me through. "Not necessary. That comment just answered my question." I narrow my eyes. "Seriously though, why are you here? And why is your shop closed?"

"I'm here to help. I've been told once or twice I know my way around a kitchen." He shrugs. "As for the bakery, I've decided to close it."

"Forever?"

He nods. "Forever."

My brows furrow in confusion. "But...why?"

"Hey, Caroline?" Ethan calls. "Do you mind giving us a minute?"

Caroline wipes her hands on a towel and grabs the tray of vegan cupcakes she's just finished decorating. "Not at all. I need to put these out front anyway."

Ethan waits for Caroline to leave the room before stepping closer to me. "I meant what I said yesterday. I'm not going anywhere. I let you go once and I have no intention of doing it again."

I glare. "You didn't *let* me go. You *shoved* me out of your life."

He winces. "I know. And it was the biggest mistake I've ever made. I allowed my emotions to guide me back then—and yes, maybe a little bit of it was ego—but I was wrong. So fucking wrong. I'm sorry for doubting you, for treating you like shit, for taking two fucking years to come to my senses. For everything, Gabbie. And I'm going to do whatever it takes to prove that to you. Shutting down the bakery was my first step in doing that."

I flinch when he cups my jaw, but I don't move out of the way. "Ethan, I—"

He places his index finger over my lips. "Hold on. I'm not done. My publicist is trying to track down the real person that sold the footage of us in your dressing room. Not because I need proof, but because I want to clear your name."

I shake my head. "I don't care about that. I

don't want to draw attention to myself again, even if your intention is honorable. The story's dead now. I'd rather keep it that way."

"Well, then do what you want with it when we get a name." Ethan brushes his thumb against my cheek. "Go out with me. Give me a chance to prove myself."

My eyes are downcast, unable to meet his gaze. "Ethan, I can't just forget everything that's happened."

Ethan lifts my chin with his finger. "I'm not asking you to. I'm just asking for another shot. I'll make it right, Gabbie."

Our eyes lock, dark brown to light blue, and we just stare for a moment. I know I might regret this, but I think I would regret it more if I didn't try.

I sigh. "Fine. One date. But don't make me regret this."

He smiles so widely, his whole face lights up. "Baby, when you see what I have planned, regret will be the last thing on your mind."

CHAPTER TWENTY-ONE

NOW

ETHAN

"This is the first time I've ever had to say this in my career, but I owe you a huge apology."

I look up as my publicist, Avery, tosses a folder in front of me. When she called earlier, telling me she had an update for me about the sex tape scandal, she insisted we meet in person. I was already at the coffee shop right by my house in Malibu so she drove straight here.

I pull out the picture of a woman that seems to have been taken with a long-range lens. She looks familiar but I can't quite place her. "Why am I looking at this?"

Avery takes the seat in front of me and gestures to the photo. "Besides the shorter hair, she bears an awfully strong resemblance to Gabriela Martinez, doesn't she?"

I study the woman in the picture. I can easily spot the differences between the two women, but then again, I have every curve of Gabbie's body memorized. To someone who doesn't, I can definitely see where they could be mistaken for one another.

"Who is this?"

"Maria Sánchez," Avery replies. "Does that name ring a bell?"

My eyes widen as I finally place her. "Shit. As in Jay Caruso's assistant?"

Avery smiles. "Exactly. Getting into Gabbie's dressing room wouldn't be a problem because a director's assistant would have free rein in the studio. Look at the signed statement."

I glance over the notarized statement from the paparazzo involved. He swears that the woman in the picture was the person who gave the footage to him and that she identified herself as Gabriela Martinez at the time.

"Holy fuck."

"We still have no motive, though. Your guess is as good as mine on that. For all we know, the whole thing was an inside job to drive publicity. That seems a bit far-fetched for a baking competition, but you never know. I've seen people in this industry do much worse for some really stupid reasons. The P.I. that I hired can dig deeper if you want. I told him to hold off until I spoke with you."

I wave the picture in the air. "Fuck, Avery. I slept with this woman. We were at a launch party a few years ago, and after a few too many drinks, had a meaningless hookup. I hadn't seen her once between then and when *Baking Masters* began filming. She started hitting on me our first day on set but I told her I wasn't interested in a repeat. She kept trying—pretty aggressively at that—until I finally told her I was seeing someone exclusively."

Avery raises a perfectly sculpted brow. "When was that?"

I think about it for a moment. "About a week before the video came out."

She rolls her eyes. "Jesus, Ethan. Your dick got you into this whole mess?"

I groan and scrub a hand over my face. "I don't know for sure, but it certainly seems like it."

"Do you want the P.I. to keep digging?"

"Let me talk to Gabbie and see what she wants to do. When I told her I was looking into it, she told me she didn't want the media attention that would arise from bringing it up again."

Avery tilts her head to the side. "She doesn't want to clear her name publicly?"

I shake my head. "She said the important people in her life know the truth and that's all that matters. Gabbie has no interest in ever being on TV again so she'd rather let the story stay buried."

Avery crosses her legs. "Huh. I can't say I see that too often."

I smile. "One of the many reasons she's such an extraordinary woman."

"You really like her, don't you?"

"She's *it* for me, Ave. We both know I've dated more than enough women over the last two years, trying to find that spark again. I've never had this kind of connection with anyone else. I may not have all the answers but that's one thing I'm sure of."

"Do you think she returns your feelings? Because whether or not she wants the media attention, it's bound to happen once you two are seen together. You, my friend, are still very much in the public eye. She has to be prepared for the speculation, Ethan. We need to make a formal statement if the vultures attack."

I think about our most recent kiss. And that really hot night in her kitchen a couple months ago. Gabbie and I have always connected on more than a physical level but it's even more pronounced when we're intimate. I felt it the first time we were together, the last time, and every time in between. Whether she's ready to admit it or not, that's one thing that hasn't changed between us.

They say there's a thin line between love and hate. I never understood that phrase more than I do now. Most of my anger with Gabbie was birthed from hurt, because my feelings for her ran so deep. I'm almost certain she'd say the same about me.

"I think so." I release a deep breath. "Only one way to find out."

"I feel like you're brewing something big, and as your publicist, a heads up would be nice."

I laugh. "Oh, it's big. But I'm not saying a word until I get everything together. I don't want to jinx it."

Avery narrows her eyes. "Since when are you superstitious?"

"I'm not," I say with a shrug. "Not really, anyway. But I don't want to risk doing anything that could ruin this for me. I can't lose her again."

She sighs. "So, what happens now?"

Gabbie refused to let me help at Sweet Temptations—I don't think I've quite convinced her I wouldn't sabotage the product—but that doesn't mean I haven't offered. After she rejected me for the third day in a row, I decided to give her the space she needed. She may have agreed to go out with me but she's been finding excuses to brush me off in the week since. I'm not letting that deter me though. I have plenty of things to keep me occupied right now, most of which involve earning her forgiveness. This groveling stuff isn't for pussies, that's for damn sure. It's hard work when you're determined to do it right.

"Now, I get my girl back."

CHAPTER TWENTY-TWO

GABBIE

"You're really giving me the silent treatment?"

Ethan's jaw clenches as he sits stoically, waiting for our makeup artist to finish wielding her magic. Normally, he doesn't need it, but our director took one look at him and commanded Ethan to head to makeup and not come back until he didn't look like he'd been on a two-day bender. Poor Crystal has her work cut out for her today. She just spent an hour with me trying to hide the fact that I was up all night crying on my best friend's shoulder. From the looks of it, Ethan's dealing with the situation by drowning himself in whiskey.

I sigh. "You don't want to know the truth? After everything, you don't want to hear what I have to say?"

Our eyes meet in the mirror. He rolls his neck

before speaking. "The *truth* is that you're a traitorous whore. That's all I need to know."

My jaw drops. "Excuse me?!"

Crystal gasps and drops her makeup sponge. "Uh...I'm gonna give you guys a few minutes." She scurries out of the room as fast as possible, slamming the door behind her.

Ethan stands up and levels me with a glare. "You fucking heard me, Gabbie. I have no interest in hearing more of your lies. If you insist on opening those pretty red lips, I'd much rather have you on your knees, choking on my cock. I mean, Luke was obviously okay that you were fucking me while you were with him. I'm sure he wouldn't mind if you blew me once more for old time's sake."

My fists clench. "Fuck. You."

He scoffs. "Nah. Been there. Done that."

I can feel my face redden. "So, this is how it's going to be?"

He backs me against the wall and crouches down until we're eye to eye. "This is how it fucking *is*. Don't look at me. Don't talk to me. Don't even *think* about me. If we're not filming, I don't fucking exist to you. After we wrap this season, I never want to see your duplicitous face again."

With that, he storms out of the room. And out of my life.

CHAPTER TWENTY-THREE

GABBIE

"So, let me get this straight." Lila takes a sip of her wine. "You agreed to go on a date with him but then you changed your mind?"

"I didn't change my mind," I shrug. "It's more like I'm stalling."

Lila tilts her head to the side. "Why?"

I take a huge bite off of a mozzarella stick and finish chewing before I reply. "I don't know."

She gives me a look that says *bullshit*. "C'mon, Gabs, you do know. You're just not willing to admit it."

I wave a piece of fried zucchini at her. What can I say; these situations call for copious amounts of carbohydrates. Might as well take advantage of happy hour pricing. "Why don't you just tell me then, since you seem to be the all-knowing?"

Lila rolls her eyes. "You're scared."

"That's ridiculous," I scoff.

"No, it's not. You don't want to be hurt again, and you're afraid that if you let him back into your life, there's a strong possibility that will happen."

"Can you blame me?" I say through a mouthful of gooey cheese.

Lila's face softens. "No, honey, I can't. But you said it yourself earlier—if you don't try, you're always going to be wondering what if. From what you've told me, he sounds genuinely repentant. Shutting down Baldwin's is *huge*, Gabbie. God, think about the monetary loss alone. He wouldn't have done that if he wasn't determined to atone for his actions."

"I know," I agree. "I just can't stop thinking about how perfect things used to be and how quickly the rug was pulled out from under me. What guarantee do I have that it won't happen again?"

"There are no guarantees. I'm not saying that you shouldn't be cautious. But if you don't try...are you willing to live with that? Humans are flawed. They make mistakes. Ethan made a *colossal* one. Regardless, he's the only man you've ever wanted a future with. He's the only man you've ever had explosive chemistry with. When things were good between you two, they were *great*. Don't you want to see if you can rekindle that?"

"He was so *cruel* to me, Lila. That last month of filming was the most difficult time in my life. The public conjecture was bad enough. But sitting next to him all day, being treated as if I were invisible...it was so painful, I could hardly breathe. I can't ever forget that feeling."

"You don't have to forget," she says and shrugs. "But you do need to ask yourself if you can *forgive*."

"I don't know," I answer honestly. "But...as much as I hate admitting this...I'm pretty sure I won't forgive *myself* if I don't try."

CHAPTER TWENTY-FOUR

NOW

ETHAN

After my publicist's reminder that we have no chance of avoiding the media if Gabbie gives me another shot, I figured I'd test the waters a bit by using the public entrance. The line of people is at least forty deep, and as I had anticipated, my arrival has caused a stir, if the whispers are any indication.

I wink at the blonde in the front of the line, who seems to be having trouble deciding what she'd like. "Get the triple chocolate cupcake. It's my favorite."

"Uh...okay." The woman turns to Gabbie, who is standing behind the counter, looking a little dumbfounded. "I'll take two please."

"Sure," Gabbie says, as she attempts to busy herself by ringing the lady up. She takes the bakery box from Caroline and passes it to the customer. "Enjoy. Have a great day."

The woman smiles. "Thanks. You too."

Caroline gives Gabbie a gentle shove and takes over the register. I follow as Gabbie walks the length of the counter until she gets to the end.

"What are you doing here, Ethan?"

I lean over and match her tone. "Why are we whispering, Gabbie?"

She looks to the side, fidgeting with the ties on her apron as she sees at least a dozen people surreptitiously staring back at us. Gabbie straightens her spine and pastes on a fake smile. "What can I do for you, Mr. Baldwin?"

I smirk. "Well, *Gabbie*...you owe me a date but you've been so swamped running this amazing bakery of yours, we haven't been able to nail down any plans. I thought I'd come by so we can at least set a date and time." I wink. "I'll figure out the rest."

Her eyes widen. "Can we talk about this later?"

"Nope." I grin. "What's the matter, Gabs? You've already said yes to the date. Why not tell me when you're available to go on said date?" I turn to the audience we've gathered, who aren't even trying to hide their fascination at this point. Some are even holding up their phones, undoubtedly recording this. "She's hesitating because I've been a real asshole when she did absolutely nothing to deserve it. But don't you think she should give me a chance to make it up to her? I'm really, *really* sorry and I give good grovel."

"What are you waiting for, honey?" a woman in line shouts. "Tell the man you'll see him tonight."

Gabbie's bronzed cheeks take on a pinkish hue. "Why are you doing this?" She's whispering again. "You're making a spectacle!"

I shrug. "Desperate times call for desperate measures."

She narrows her eyes. "Fine. Tonight."

"Great! I'll pick you up at six." I dig my phone out of my pocket and place it on the counter in front of her. "I haven't been to your new place yet, so I'll need your address."

What she doesn't know is that the P.I. I hired already got that information for me. If she tries giving me a fake, I'll know it.

She stabs the phone with her fingers a few times and passes it back to me. I quickly glance at the address she gave me before pocketing it again. I'll take it as a good sign that she typed in the real one.

"Fine. See you at six," she grumbles.

Gabbie stiffens when I lean over the glass case to place a chaste kiss on her cheek. I hover for just a moment before whispering in her ear so no one else can hear. "I look forward to it, Gabs. Wear something sexy. Underwear is optional."

I laugh as I pull back and see the sheer rage in her eyes. I have no doubt that if we didn't have witnesses right now, she'd be jumping over this counter to strangle me. I have to consciously make an effort to fight an erection because angry Gabbie is fucking hot. She's still shooting daggers at me when I give her a little wave before ducking out the door.

Damn, tonight's going to be fun.

CHAPTER TWENTY-FIVE

GABBIE

God, I hope I'm not making a mistake. It's not like Ethan gave me much of a choice with that damn show he put on earlier. I have Google alerts set up, tracking any news regarding the bakery, and sure enough, shortly after Ethan left, footage of our encounter was streaming across the internet from various people's cell phones.

They're postulating several different scenarios, all trying to decode Ethan's remark about treating me poorly without merit. And of course, just what I didn't want to happen, did, in fact, happen, when those gossip sites mentioned the incident from two years ago. Thankfully, they're not vicious in nature yet; some are even suggesting the events were somehow misconstrued. Ha! You can say that again.

It's ten before six and I'm a nervous wreck. Ethan's demand to dress sexy irked me so I decided to do just the opposite out of spite. It might not be the most mature approach, but you can't say he didn't ask for it. Besides, I don't really own anything frumpy; I just made sure to cover as much skin as possible, weather permitting. I walk to the full-length mirror in my bedroom and take in my chosen outfit for the evening. I'm wearing a high-neck sleeveless green blouse, black capris, and my favorite strappy sandals. This should work whether we go somewhere casual or fancy and as a bonus, Ethan's eyes won't have any cleavage to feast on.

I take a look around the open space, wondering how it would appear through Ethan's eyes. My décor is shabby chic, which is fitting for a beach cottage, but I have accent pieces scattered about that reflect my heritage. My father wasn't in the picture so my mother moved to California when she was six months pregnant, wanting a better life for me than she could provide in Mexico. She moved into a tiny apartment with my *tía* Rosa, which is where I spent the first eighteen years of my life. We didn't have much, but we were happy.

Growing up poor gave me an extra level of appreciation for everything that I've achieved as an adult. It made me work harder to get where I am today. I'll never forget the look on their faces when I signed several endorsement deals and bought my aunt and mother a new house. I'm certainly not wealthy; in fact, most of the income from my brief stint at the Cooking Network was funneled into my bakery. But as long as business continues to do okay, I'm not struggling, and that's all I really need.

They say opposites attract but Ethan and I take that to the extreme, besides our mutual love for food. One thing I've learned about creative types though, is that people who are passionate about their craft are typically passionate in most areas of their lives. That rule certainly applies to us. Whether it's our tempers, excitement about creating a new dessert, or yes, even sexually, we have passion in spades. Is that really enough though?

Just as I'm freshening my poppy red lip stain, my doorbell rings. I live in a tiny Spanish bungalow so it only takes me a few seconds to reach the front door and check the peephole. Ethan is standing on my front stoop, looking directly at me, as if he knows I'm watching him. I turn the locks and pull on the heavy wooden door.

I purposely stand over the threshold, blocking his entry. "You're early."

His arm comes from behind his back, producing a giant bouquet of Casablanca lilies. "I couldn't wait any longer to see you."

I grab the flowers from him and inhale their

unique fragrance. I don't recall ever telling him these were my favorites so it was either a coincidence, or Ethan's been doing some digging. I'd put my money on the latter.

I'm not going to let perfectly good flowers wilt, so I begrudgingly step aside to let him in. "Thank you. Let me put these in water and we can go."

The door closes behind him as he follows me inside the house. I dig through a cabinet to find something big enough to hold the bouquet and glance over at Ethan through the corner of my eye. He's a large man so his presence is a bit overwhelming in my nine hundred square foot cottage.

"Nice place, Gabbie."

"Thanks. I bought it about a year ago. There's just two bedrooms and one bath, but I'm only a mile from the beach so I can't complain." I place the lilies in a vase and set them on the small dining table. "Are you still at that place in Brentwood?"

Ethan shakes his head. "Nah. It's actually an investment property now. I bought a place in Malibu overlooking the ocean."

"Of course you did," I mutter.

See what I mean about our differences? Between that and our tumultuous past, I should just quit while I'm ahead.

He narrows his eyes. "What's that supposed to mean?"

I blow out a breath. "Look, Ethan. I don't think this is such a great idea. Maybe we should just—"

I lose my train of thought when his full lips brush against mine with a featherlike touch. "Maybe we should *what*, Gabs?"

I shake my head, trying to recall what I was saying. This is too much. My brain is too clouded. Hard, assertive Ethan I can handle. Soft, gentle Ethan confuses the hell out of me. The fog in my head thickens as he begins trailing light kisses down the side of my neck.

"I—" My fingernails dig into his bicep when he nips my earlobe. "I don't remember."

He smiles against my skin. "Fight it all you want, Gabbie, but this is going to happen. You *want* me."

Well, that cleared the haze. Cocky bastard. At least his ego is good for something.

I shove him away. "Keep your lips to yourself, mister. I am *not* having sex with you."

Ethan barks out a laugh. "So, that's how we're going to play this? Why are you denying what we both want?"

I glare. "This isn't a game. This is my *life*. And I'm not denying anything. I never said I didn't want you. But I don't *want* to want you. Nothing good can come from this, Ethan."

If I'm not mistaken, actual hurt flashes across

his face. "I see. Well, I'll just have to work harder at changing your mind then."

I cross my arms over my chest. "And how do you plan on doing that?"

He flashes his golden boy smile. "You'll see."

CHAPTER TWENTY-SIX

NOW

ETHAN

I shift my car into park. "We're here."

Gabbie blinks a few times, watching the surf crashing on the beach. "You brought me to the beach?"

"That is what people usually call places with sand and water."

She turns toward me and glares. "You don't need to be such a smartass about it."

I exit my car, round the front, and open Gabbie's door with exaggerated flourish. "Come on out, Gabs. I won't bite." I pull her into my body when she takes my hand and add, "Unless you want me to."

Gabbie pushes off me, rolling her eyes. "Well, one thing hasn't changed. You're still arrogant as fuck."

I laugh as I open the trunk, grabbing the bags I had packed. "I prefer the term *confident*."

Her lips turn up in the corner, as if she's fighting a smile. "I'm sure."

I take her hand, quite frankly surprised she doesn't pull it back, and lead her out onto the beach. We walk in silence, as the sun slowly ebbs toward the sea. I couldn't have timed this any better. The place is practically empty, except for a few surfers in the water, and the temperature is starting to cool. Not enough to be uncomfortable, but hopefully enough that she'll want me to warm her up later.

I nod to a spot right next to a lifeguard tower. "How about right here?"

"Sure."

I dig the blanket out of my bag and spread it out, gesturing for her to sit. I spread another one over her legs and take my place next to her.

I turn my body inward and tuck a stray hair behind her ear. "You okay with this?"

Gabbie inches back a little, breaking the contact, and eyes me thoughtfully. "Depends on what you have planned."

I widen my eyes in mock innocence. "Why, dinner, of course."

I pull out several insulated containers. One by one, I reveal my offerings. Enchiladas *suizas* from her favorite Mexican restaurant, a selection of artisan cheeses to go with the bottle of chardonnay she loves, and a special dessert from this great little bakery.

Gabbie's eyes widen as she points at the last dish accusingly. "How did you get *that*?"

I wink. "I may have paid someone standing in the back of the line earlier to grab them for me."

She snatches the signature pink box out of my hands, staring down at the logo imprinted on top. "What's in it?"

"Open it and find out."

Gabbie lifts the flap and raises the cardboard lid. I stifle a groan as her beautiful red lips widen in a smile, because I'm now imagining them wrapped around my cock.

"I was so bummed when I sold the last two. I *really* wanted to take one home after we closed."

I lift the chocolate-dipped cannoli from the box and press it against her lips. "There's no reason we can't start with dessert."

She swallows hard before parting her lips and taking a bite out of the crispy shell. Gabbie shamelessly releases a moan as she chews, making my dick stand up and take notice. Christ, I need the damn sun to go down before I get arrested for indecent exposure.

When she finishes chewing, I wipe a little ricotta

from the corner of her mouth and press my thumb against her lips. "Open."

My nostrils flare as she parts her lips just enough to take the tip of my thumb inside her mouth. I can't muffle the groan this time as her tongue swirls around, licking it clean.

"Jesus fuck, Gabbie."

My words seem to snap her out of a haze as she releases me and scoots back some more. "I shouldn't have done that."

"Why not?" I look around pointedly. "No one's around to see us."

She shakes her head. "I meant it when I said I'm not sleeping with you, Ethan. You need to play fair."

Play fair, my ass. This woman wants me just as much as I want her. Her pupils are dilated, her nipples are poking through the thin top she's wearing, and her breaths are shallow. I understand why she has reservations but if I'm being honest, it's frustrating as fuck. I've never been known for my patience, but with her, it's even worse. I wasted two fucking years already; I don't want to wait another second.

I clear my throat and reach for the two plastic cups I brought with me. "Hold these for a sec, will you?"

Gabbie eyes me warily as she grabs them from me. "Did you hear what I said, Ethan?"

I uncork the bottle and fill each cup generously. "I heard you. I just don't agree with you so I thought it'd be best to keep my mouth shut."

She snorts in the most adorable yet sexy way. "Well, at least you're honest."

I look her right in the eye. "I've never been anything but honest with you, Gabbie."

She lifts a brow. "Even when you called me a traitorous whore?"

"Okay." I stretch out the word and scrub a hand over my face. "You wanna do this now, huh?"

Gabbie waves her hand through the air. "Might as well get it over with. We're past the point of niceties, Ethan. I don't think either one of us can truly move on without airing our grievances and hearing the other person's side of the story."

"Right." I take a fortifying breath. "Look, I felt like a complete asshole the moment those words left my mouth, and I couldn't possibly regret them any more than I do, but you've gotta understand, I was going out of my mind. I spent practically all night drinking myself into a stupor, thinking that you and Luke were together, laughing about what a fool I'd been." I wince as the memory sharpens. "As time went on, I couldn't erase those thoughts from my brain and I kept getting flashes of us in bed together—*really graphic fucking images*—but then *I* would morph into *him*. Every. Damn. Time. I literally thought I was going crazy for a while there."

Gabbie drinks half her glass in one gulp. "The same thing happened to me whenever I saw you in the tabloids with a new actress or model on your arm. Many, *many*, different actresses and models. You didn't seem so distraught then."

I shake my head. "That's because that's what I wanted you to see, on the slim chance you were still paying attention."

"I was *always* paying attention," she admits so quietly, I can barely hear her voice over the waves.

I bump my shoulder into hers. "I would've done the same, but you just disappeared. After you left the studio, and the story died down, I couldn't find any news about you. Believe me, I fucking *tried*. Then, one day about a year later, I actually saw you on the street. You were coming out of that café right next to the pier. *Holding Luke Warner's hand*. I couldn't fucking believe it.

"I didn't even think about what I did next. I followed you. You walked back to the bakery—that's how I found out about it. I watched as he kissed you goodbye and left with a huge grin on his face. When he noticed me standing there like a schmuck, that asshole's smile got even bigger. All of the anger I felt before came back with a vengeance. It took everything in me not to punch him right in his smug face."

"Are you sure he saw you? He never said a word to me."

I clench my jaw. "Oh, he saw me. As he was walking past me, that prick actually said, 'Thanks for fucking up, Baldwin, because now I've got the girl and I plan on keeping her.'"

Gabbie chugs the rest of her wine and holds her cup out, asking for more. "I remember that day. He was acting really weird that night. Now I know why."

Since I have the perfect segue, I ask the question that's been plaguing me for too long. "Was it serious? You said you started dating about six months after...after everything went down. How long did it last?"

She pops a cube of cheese in her mouth and finishes chewing before answering me. "You really want to hear this?"

No, but I think I need to. "We're getting it all out there, right?"

"Right." She bites her lip while appearing to collect her thoughts. "He was there for me when I needed someone. We were friends first and it just naturally developed into...*more*. We were exclusive, and it was comfortable, but it was always missing something. There was no spark...at least on my end. I actually broke it off about a week after you saw us because I realized that I loved him as a friend, but I wasn't *in* love with him. It wasn't fair to either of us if I pretended otherwise."

I exhale, digesting everything she just shared

with me. I fucking hate that they were together—I always will—but I really have no one to blame but myself for that. If I would've just calmed the hell down long enough to listen to her back then, we would've never gone our separate ways. I practically drove her into his arms. Hindsight really is a nasty bitch.

"Do you still talk to him?"

She gives me a sad smile. "No. I wanted to remain friends but he didn't. He *was* in love with me and said he couldn't go backwards. It was all or nothing for him."

"Stupid son of a bitch." Can't say I blame him, though. I could never be just friends with this woman after knowing what it's like being with her. I also can't say that I'm not thrilled he's no longer in the picture.

She playfully punches my shoulder. "What about you and your loooooong list of ladies?"

I point to the sun as it's just about to set. "Look."

We watch in silence as it dips below the horizon. Gabbie releases a sigh, making me think about all the times she did that for an entirely different reason.

She pinches my forearm to get my attention. "Don't think you're getting out of answering the question, Baldwin."

I shrug. "There's nothing to tell, really. I dated, but nothing ever evolved into a relationship. They were more of a distraction than anything."

Gabbie gives me a wry look. "How lovely of you to use all those women as a *distraction*."

I raise my eyebrows. "Trust me, it was mutual. They knew I wasn't looking for anything serious from the start."

"Why not?"

Now I give her the wry look. "I was a bit jaded. And even though I didn't consciously recognize it at the time, there was only *one woman* I wanted to be with and she wasn't an option."

Gabbie sits on that for a moment before lifting the enchilada box and inhaling the incredible aroma wafting from it. She gasps and mutters something in Spanish. "Holy shit! Are these from *Casa Colima*?"

I smile. "They are."

"How did you know?"

"I may have had a little insider info."

She narrows her eyes. "Dammit, Caroline."

I laugh. "Not Caroline, actually. Your friend, Lila. I recognized her when I stopped by my realtor's office the other day and asked her to help me out."

"That bitch," she mutters, although there's no venom behind her words. "She didn't tell me."

"That's because I told her about this project I have going and she likes what I have planned. If it makes you feel better, she did threaten to castrate me if I fucked up again."

"What project?"

I wink. "You'll find out soon enough."

CHAPTER TWENTY-SEVEN

GABBIE

"Hello?"

"Is this Gabriela Martinez?"

I hold the phone with my shoulder so I can unlock my front door. "This is she."

"Hi, my name is Cheryl Iverson from First California Title. When would be a good time for you to come in and sign papers?"

"*What* papers?"

Cheryl clears her throat. "For the deed transfer on the property located at 1303 Ocean Front Walk, suite 106."

What the hell?

"I'm sorry Ms. Iverson, you must be mistaken. I own suite 105, not 106, and I can assure you, I have no intention of selling to anyone." There's silence on the other end of the line. "Hello? Are you there?"

"Yes, I'm here." I can hear papers shuffling. "I'm sorry if I wasn't clear before. The documents I have involve transferring ownership of suite 106 *to* you from Baldwin's Bakery Enterprises."

I frown. "I'm not looking to buy any property either."

"You don't understand, Ms. Martinez, this is a zero-value transaction, meaning no funds will be exchanged. Mr. Baldwin is *gifting* the property to you. He's hired my office to secure all necessary signatures and file the gift deed with the county. It's pretty clear but I can double check with my lead escrow officer if you'd like."

I'm so stunned, I drop my purse and keys on the ground right inside my entryway. "Uh...no, that won't be necessary, but can I get back to you on that appointment?"

"Sure. We're here Monday through Friday from eight to six."

I end the call and lean against the door for support. After our date the other night, in which he was surprisingly understanding about why I wouldn't let him inside after we got back to my house, Ethan told me to expect a surprise within the next couple of days. I thought he meant flowers or something, not commercial real estate!

What in the world is he up to? I scroll through

my contacts until I find his name and press the call button.

"Hello, beautiful," he answers.

I jump straight to the point. "What the hell are you doing, Ethan?"

"Well, right this very minute, I'm walking up to your front door."

"What?!"

He chuckles. "Open the door, Gabbie."

I end the call and take a few deep breaths before opening the door, finding Ethan on my front stoop with a shit-eating grin. I don't give him a chance to enter. Instead, I step outside and shut the door behind me.

"Why is a title company calling me, asking me to sign papers so you can transfer ownership of your property to me?"

"Oh, that." I swear I'm two seconds away from smacking that look off his face. "That's my surprise."

I throw my hands up. "You can't just *give* me a million-dollar piece of property!"

"It's valued at three-point-two million actually, but that's irrelevant."

"What do you mean *that's irrelevant?*" I'm shrieking at this point but I can't seem to stop myself. "You can't just give me something like that!"

"Why not?"

I pinch the bridge of my nose. "*Dios mío*, you're going to drive me *loca*."

"Ooh, say that again. You know I love it when you get all fired up and start rambling in Spanish." He winks.

"*Pinche pendejo*," I mutter, narrowing my eyes for emphasis.

Ethan's deep laugh rumbles through me. "You can call me an asshole all you want, Gabs, but I'm still going to think it's sexy coming from your mouth."

"Ethan, will you be serious for a minute?" I sigh.

"Who said I'm not being serious?" He gestures toward the house. "C'mon, Gabs, let me in. I really don't think this is a conversation that your neighbors need to hear."

I groan, throwing the door open and stomping inside, with Ethan right behind me. I whip around and cross my arms over my chest, to ensure he knows I mean business. "Let me try this a different way. *Why* do you think you should give me a multi-million-dollar piece of real estate? Why do you think I'd even want it?"

"I figured it would be useful if you wanted to expand the store," he shrugs. "Maybe add more kitchen space and branch out to event catering. Or have café seating and turn it into half bakery, half coffee house. The possibilities are endless, Gabbie.

If that's not something you can see yourself doing, just sell it."

"Why don't *you* just sell it?"

"Because it should've never been mine in the first place. Believe it or not, I do have a conscience and I couldn't live with the guilt if I didn't take some sort of hit on this whole mess."

I rub my temples. "What does that even mean?"

"It means that I should've never made an offer on that property. I should've never opened my bakery there. I should've never launched an attack on *your* bakery." He places his hands on my hips and leans down to speak softly in my ear. "I needed to do something big to prove how badly I regret every shitty thing I've ever done or said to you. This was the best solution I could think of since I can't change the past, no matter how much I want to."

I take a step back, unable to think clearly when his hands are pressed against me. "Ethan, I can't accept it. It's too much. Closing your store was more than enough proof."

He cringes. "Speaking of proof...there's something I didn't get to share with you the other night."

I head over to the couch and take a seat. I'm fairly certain I should be sitting down for whatever he's about to say. "What now?"

"I know who's responsible for the video."

My eyes widen. "Who?"

"Jay Caruso's assistant, Maria."

"Why would she do that? And how do you know?"

He sits next to me and turns his body so we're facing each other. "We have a sworn statement from the guy who sold it, identifying her. My publicist says it could've been a publicity stunt, but jealously was the more probable motive. She can have the P.I. keep digging if you want to know for sure."

"Why would jealousy be a motive?"

He clears his throat and rubs the back of his neck. "We...uh...hooked up once, about a year before we started filming *Baking Masters*. When she saw me on set, she made it pretty clear she wanted a repeat. I told her I wasn't interested but she kept coming on to me.

"It got to the point where she was starting to give me major stalker vibes so I admitted that I was seeing someone exclusively. I didn't tell her *who* I was seeing, but I made it painfully obvious that I had no intention of letting you go. She said she understood then pretended like I didn't even exist. Or so I thought, anyway. That all happened only about a week before the footage was released."

"You've got to be kidding me, Ethan! My reputation was trashed and my entire life was uprooted because one of your past exploits felt scorned?"

He frowns. "I don't know for certain, but it makes the most sense."

I can't believe this. Everything I went through

was because some crazy woman couldn't handle rejection. I'm so pissed right now; I don't even know what to say. If I gave Ethan another shot, who's to say this wouldn't happen again?

"Don't do that." He grabs my hand, his desperation palpable. "I know what you're thinking right now and I swear to you nothing like this would ever happen again. I'm a man who learns from his mistakes. I'm by no means perfect, but I swear to you, Gabbie, I will never do anything to hurt you again."

I want to believe him. I really do. But I don't know if I can.

I sigh. "Ethan, I need time to process."

He groans. "We've already wasted two years. Giving you time is only going to give you a chance to talk yourself out of this."

"That's not true." I shake my head to emphasize my point.

He places his hands on each side of my jaw, forcing me to look at him. "Yes, it is. And I'm not going to let you do this. You said yourself, you wanted to keep the past in the past. So, why can't we start over? Why can't you give me a chance and take it day by day?"

I search his eyes. "It's not that simple."

"It can be."

I look away. "No, it can't. That's not how this works."

Ethan pinches my chin between his thumb and forefinger, searching my eyes. "Do you love me?"

His question is so unexpected, the words tumble out of me, without any regard for consequences. "I never stopped."

His brilliant smile disarms me. I can practically feel the wall around my heart crumbling as a pressure I didn't realize existed rises from my chest.

Ethan's index finger traces the length of my jaw. "Then we'll figure out the rest. *Together.*"

Lust punches me in the gut when Ethan's lips press against mine. Logic wages a war with my body's visceral reaction to him. I straddle his lap without thought and moan when his large hands press against my back, effectively smashing my breasts against his chest. God, why do his lips have to be so perfect? Why does everything feel so damn right when he's kissing me? So many thoughts are on the tip of my tongue, yet I say nothing because desire has taken the helm.

Ethan breaks our kiss and groans when I slide my core back and forth over his denim-clad cock. "This is what you do to me, Gabbie. This is what you've *always* done to me. But that's not all we are and you know it. This thing between us has *never* been just physical."

I whimper as his thumbs brush over my nipples, the lace of my bra abrading the stiff peaks. "I'm scared."

He kisses a trail down the side of my face, chasing the lone tear that escaped. "I know, baby. But I swear on my fucking life that I will do everything in my power to make you happy. Because living without you anymore isn't an option for me. Please say you'll be mine, Gabs."

I rest my palms on either side of his face. "I've been yours since the day we met."

His sexy, signature smirk is on full blast. "Thank fuck, because if I'm not inside you in the next five minutes, my dick may actually explode."

I stand up and offer my hand. "Well, we certainly can't let that happen. I have plans for that thing."

He chuckles as I lead him down the hall to my bedroom. "Do tell."

Once inside my room, I step out of my yoga pants and remove my shirt. "I'd rather show you."

Ethan bites his knuckles as I slowly unclasp my bra. "I fucking love that idea."

My breath hitches when his muscles bunch beneath his fitted tee. This man is unequivocally masculine yet unquestionably beautiful. Every single part of me bolts to attention as his crystalline eyes bore into my exposed flesh. My skin flushes as he languidly peruses my body, pausing briefly over my breasts before meeting my gaze.

I have to remind myself to breathe as I shrug

the straps off my shoulders and step out of my panties. "I thought you might."

Ethan sheds his clothing faster than I would've thought possible and lunges into action. Our mouths meet again in a savage union of greed and desire and an overwhelming need to make up for lost time. Our hands are everywhere they can reach. Our kisses are filled with promise.

Ethan and I become a frenzy of movement, unable to decide if we want fast and hard or soft and slow. The only certainty is my surrender to his touch. To my irrepressible longing. To the feeling that only this man can ignite. I'm long past the point of dwelling on the past or worrying about the future.

As Ethan slides his thick length into my body, all I know is that right here, right now, everything is as it should be. I revel in the sensations, that all-consuming burn as he moves inside of me. I'm arching and moaning as he establishes an unrelenting rhythm, taking my body to heights that only he can achieve. Our skin is slicked with sweat, my body heated one second and covered in goose bumps the next.

Desperation tears through me as the telltale signs of ecstasy surface. With a few more measured thrusts, I'm free falling into delirium. When my inner muscles stop contracting around him, Ethan holds nothing back. He renews his pace, owning my pleasure and my heart and my mind. Everything I have to give is his to take.

My name surges from his lips as he reaches completion. A few more pumps and then he stills. Ethan lazily sucks my nipple into his mouth before resting his forehead against my chest, our ragged breaths the only sound in the room. I thread my fingers through his thick, dark hair and bask in the peacefulness of this moment.

After a moment, he withdraws, and pulls me into his side. He strokes my hair, making me drowsy. Right before he lulls me to sleep, Ethan hugs me closer and says the words that I've been longing to hear.

"I love you, Gabriela. It's always been you and it will never be anyone *but* you."

A smile forms on my lips as I snuggle into him and groggily echo the sentiment. As I'm drifting off to dreamland, I think to myself how perfect this feels being in Ethan's arms. We've had some major bumps along the way, and I'm sure we'll face some more down the road, but the one thing I know for certain, is there's no one else I'd rather have by my side.

EPILOGUE

2 YEARS LATER

ETHAN

I don't know if I've ever been this nervous in my entire life. Ever since Gabriela Martinez came back into my world, I've been happier than I ever thought possible. That's not just my dick talking either, although, make no mistake, he is *very* happy. Gabbie challenges me, personally and professionally. She makes me laugh. She makes me envision a future that I had never wanted before I met her.

In a nutshell, she makes me want to be a better man.

Hence, the anxiety, because everything I've ever wanted is riding on her answer.

"I think I'm just about done here. There's just one more thing that's bothering me." I take her hand as we exit my flagship store.

Gabbie looks at me questioningly. "What's that?"

I gesture to the sign hanging above the bakery. I invited her to Las Vegas on the pretense that I needed to check on this place, but I have something more personal in mind as well. "That sign isn't working for me. I think I need to revamp it."

She scrunches her nose. "I think it looks great. Why would you want to change it?"

I shrug, feigning nonchalance. "It's missing something."

"Like what?"

I pull out my phone and scroll through the pictures until I reach the mockup I had made. "Something like this."

I watch Gabbie's expression as she looks over the photo. A deep crease forms between her brows as she appears to be trying to make sense of what she's seeing. "Baldwin's Sweet Temptations." She shakes her head in confusion. "I don't understand."

Gabbie's business has been booming since she decided to expand into catering, but Sweet Temptations isn't really a household name outside of Southern California. It's a damn shame if you ask me because some of her signature recipes are the best damn desserts that I've ever tasted. If she agrees to this, people from around the world would know how talented she is.

I clear my throat. "What are your thoughts on a merger?"

"You want to merge our companies?"

I place my hands in my pockets, discreetly wrapping my fist around a small velvet bag. "Sure. I can only think of one loophole that we'd need to get through."

"What's that?"

Gabbie gets jostled by a small crowd passing by so she grabs on to my arm to keep herself upright. It's just after eleven in the evening so the bakery is closed, but this is Vegas, so people are still everywhere. There's a small service hallway to the left so I pull her over there to have a little more privacy.

I pull the bag out of my pocket and retrieve the custom-made ring. It's not too flashy, because that's not Gabbie's style, but it's exquisite nonetheless. She thought I was meeting with an investor but I was really at a local jewelers.

I hold up the flawless, two-carat oval-shaped solitaire. "The Baldwin part. It doesn't really work unless both owners share that name."

She taps her plump red lips with her index finger, not giving anything away. "I like that idea, all things considered."

I smirk. "*What* things considered?"

See what I mean about her constantly challenging me? I have to remind my dick this is not the time to get worked up.

She holds out her left hand, silently prompting me to slide the ring on her finger. I don't waste a second marking this woman as mine for everyone to see. "So all *three* of us could share the same name."

"I'm not following."

Gabbie raises a perfectly sculpted brow and nods to her stomach. "I couldn't let you be the only one with a surprise, Ethan."

I fall to my knees the moment it hits me and place my hands on her stomach. "You're pregnant?"

She runs her fingers through my hair. "About two months along."

"Holy shit," I whisper, placing soft kisses over her abdomen.

Gabbie stopped taking birth control a few months ago but we weren't actively trying. We both figured if it was meant to be, it would happen eventually.

"You good with that?"

"I'm fucking great with that." I stand up and kiss her hard. As I pull away, I say, "Let's get married tonight."

Dark lashes feather against her cheeks as she blinks rapidly. "Tonight?"

I smile. "Yeah, tonight. Neither one of us are into the fanfare that a big wedding would produce. Why not just go for it? There's no easier place to get hitched."

Gabbie takes my hand and returns my smile. "I can't think of anything else I'd rather do."

I couldn't agree more.

Want more sexy enemies-to-lovers stories? CLICK HERE to check out the rest of the Bedding the Billionaire series!

ALSO BY LAURA LEE

Dealing With Love Series (Interconnected standalones)

♥Deal Breakers (Devyn & Riley's story)

♥Deal Takers (Rainey & Brody's story)

♥Deal Makers (Charlotte and Drew's story)

Bedding the Billionaire Series (Interconnected standalones)

♥Billionaire Bosshole

♥Billionaire Bossman (Formerly Public Relations)

♥Billionaire Bad Boy (Formerly Sweet Temptations)

Windsor Academy Series (Books 1-3 must be read in order)

♥Wicked Liars

♥Ruthless Kings

♥Fallen Heirs

♥Broken Playboy (Bentley's story-can be read as a standalone)

Standalone Novels

♥Beautifully Broken

♥Happy New You

♥Redemption

If you'd like to be one of the first to know about new releases or sales, sign up for Laura's newsletter at:

https://www.subscribepage.com/LauraLeeBooks

ABOUT THE AUTHOR

Laura Lee is the *USA Today* bestselling author of steamy and sometimes ridiculously funny romance. She won her first writing contest at the ripe old age of nine, earning a trip to the state capital to showcase her manuscript. Thankfully for her, those early works will never see the light of day again!

Laura lives in the Pacific Northwest with her wonderful husband, two beautiful children, and three of the most poorly behaved cats in existence. She likes her fruit smoothies filled with rum, her cupboards stocked with Cadbury's chocolate, and her music turned up loud. When she's not chasing the kids around, writing, or watching HGTV, she's reading anything she can get her hands on. She's a sucker for spicy romances, especially those that can make her laugh!

For more information about the author, check out her website at: www.LauraLeeBooks.com
You can also find her "working" on social media quite frequently.

Facebook: @LauraLeeBooks1
Instagram: @LauraLeeBooks
Twitter: @LauraLeeBooks
Verve Romance: @LauraLeeBooks
Reader's Group: Laura Lee's Lounge
TikTok: @AuthorLauraLee

ACKNOWLEDGMENTS

To my husband, Tad: You're my biggest supporter, my best friend, and my partner in crime. I love you 3000.

To my children: Thank you for not fighting too much while I was locked away trying to meet this deadline. You two are my greatest gift even when you're testing my sanity.

To my lovely beta Crystal: Thank you for being the first person to read Gabbie and Ethan's story. Your feedback was invaluable.

To all the seriously awesome bloggers in the book world: I appreciate you more than words can ever say, as a reader and a writer. Thank you for all you do to help others find new book boyfriends.

To my ARC team and Loungers: Thank you for being such awesome, hilarious, and supportive ladies. Keep those Chris Hemsworth pics and GIFs coming!

To my editor, Erin Potter: Thank you once again, for polishing my work and making the final product so much better!

Last but never least, to my readers: I love sharing all the random shit that comes out of my brain with you. It's a privilege bringing stories into your life for a living.

www.ingramcontent.com/pod-product-compliance
Lightning Source LLC
Chambersburg PA
CBHW071829190726
48292CB00005B/1687